Jihadi

White Christmas

Continuing the Mark Alden adventures

A Suspense Thriller Fiction Novel

By Rik Thistle

Rik Thistle

Acknowledgements

Thank you to my family and friends who have helped me with ideas and criticisms of this continuing story. I have used some of their names either first or last, as a tribute to their friendship and their help throughout the writing and editing process. Hope you enjoy the ongoing adventure of Mark Aldin and Michelle Samaha.

Special thanks to Dr. Greg Johnson and Geoff Wilcox for their help in the editing process.

Jihadi White Christmas

For all the United States of America military men and women past and present who put their lives on the line every day to protect our way of life and freedom.

/jiˈhädē/
Noun
a person involved in a jihad; an Islamic militant

Qur'an 2:191

"Slay them wherever ye find them, and drive them out of the places whence they drove you out ... if they attack you (there) then slay them. Such is the reward of disbelievers."

Qur'an 4:74

"Fight in the way of Allah who sell the life of this world for the other. Whoso fighteth in the way of Allah, be he slain or be he victorious, on him We shall bestow a vast reward."

Rik Thistle

Copyright © 2018 by Thistle Literary LLC

Thistle Literary LLC Edition December, 2018

Manufactured in the United States of America

10 9 8 7 6 5 4 3 2 1

ISBN 979-0-578-21443-6

Chapter 1

Pyongyang North Korea
August 22nd

Kim Jong-Un is in shock. After his generals told him that the United States president's decision to attack the DPRK was imminent, the dear leader fled the Presidential palace knowing it would be one of the first targets of the American bombs. In the middle of the night Kim, his wife and three of his children are rushed out of the presidential palace and into a bullet-proof SUV. Waiting in a separate SUV are eight of Kim's personal guards. The Chairman and his key generals pile into one of his personal limousines.

Knowing that most of his military sites would be attacked, Kim makes the decision to head for a secret underground facility just forty-five miles from Pyongyang.

In the limo with Kim are his most trusted Generals. General Gim Chi-Sung is the head of the Korean People's Armed Forces. He is the key player for Kim, and the most loyal. Also included are General Ri Pyong-Chol, the person who can launch the DPRK conventional and nuclear arsenal and finally Jeong Jha-Ji who heads up the secret police. Kim knows that this will just speed up the plan he and Iran had hatched several years ago. Iran and North Korea have been working together over the past decade both helping the other to develop nuclear weapons. Both countries believed it was the only way they could survive the imperialist threat of the United States and Europe. An Iranian Revolutionary Guard general contacted General Ri about accelerating their attack on America, but now apparently the Americans have found out about their plan and decided to attack first.

"Dear leader, if we are going to launch our nuclear missiles we must to act now. If we wait, the Americans could launch first and take out our military facilities."

Kim Jong-Un is regaining some of his senses as the limo and three SUVs race out of the city. "Are we sure the Americans are planning an attack?"

General Ri nods. "We have been told by our Saudi contact who told us that his contact within the U.S. State Department confirmed that the President is committed to overthrowing North Korea and unifying Korea. They discovered our nuclear deceit and the secret nuclear development sites. Plus General Aziz with the Revolutionary Guard confirmed the information."

Kim looks absentmindedly out of the tinted window at the dark North Korean countryside as it flies past. "What do our Chinese brothers say?"

"Our Chinese *brothers* have not replied to my call." Says Jeong Jha-Ji.

Jeong Jha-Ji is the head of the secret police and is one of the most feared men in North Korea, besides Kim Jong-Un of course. "Mr. Chairman, we are running out of time. The Americans could be launching their missiles. Once they attack, all of our military facilities will be vulnerable. We need to activate the Red Guards; that will put 3.5 million workers on alert to stop the South Korea army that will invade."

Kim knows that General Ri is right but he wants to be the one to give the order. His people believe he is a god, just like his father and grandfather before him.

"I should go on television, talk directly to the people."

The Generals glance at each other; they know that only the elite and middle class in North Korea have a television. Those who do would be warned by their high level friends and family. General Ri looks at the other Generals, then says. "We do not have the cameras and systems to broadcast from facility 358." The General leans forward and lowers his voice so as to not be overheard by the driver. "We should also consider the aftermath if the Americans invade our country. We are heading to facility 358 near Anju and that will give you and your family an opportunity to leave North Korea and flee to China."

Kim Jong-Un turns his head slowly and stares at his General and hisses. "I will not leave my country! We will stop the Americans. They must not be allowed to invade. Every man, woman and child will fight to the death to push the Americans into the sea!"

The outburst quiets the Generals. After a few minutes of silence, General Ri responds, "But sir, we need to consider all possibilities. Your survival is critical to the government."

Kim sits back, calming down. "Yes of course." Kim closes his eyes considering the situation. "Alright, launch the ICBMs. When we get to facility 358 we can coordinate our forces and truly understand what the Americans are up to."

The Generals look at each other but say nothing. General Ri places a call from the limo to his second in command authorizing the launching of their twelve ballistic missiles. It will take several hours to fuel and target the missiles but the Chairman is confident they can release the nuclear storm on the Americans before they can react. The issue is the aftermath; they know that the bunker called facility 358 has subpar equipment given to them by the Russians and can barely keep up with information in real-time. The computers breakdown and spare parts are sometimes no longer available, no matter how hard they search. The Generals know they are hopelessly over-matched by the military of the United States of America, both in technology and their firepower. But disputing the Chairman could lead to a bullet in the brain as Kim Jong-Un has done to countless other military and political adversaries.

After an hour drive in silence, the limo and the trailing SUVs pull into a barbed wire compound that shows three buildings guarded by several hundred special-forces troops. As the limo rolls to a halt inside a large garage, the North Korean leader steps out to be greeted by four of the top facility military leadership. As the three Generals step out of the limo, the military leaders are shocked. They snap salutes, nervous that both the Dear Leader and his top Generals have come to their facility.

The family and the Generals are led to an elevator that takes them three hundred feet down to the underground bunker that the leadership believes will safeguard them in the event the Americans attack.

As Kim Jong-Un enters the command center, all of the personnel stand and clap. "Thank you. Everyone please take your seats and continue to monitor the events outside of our country. We are about to launch our first volley of ICBMs at the United States. What are the Americans doing?"

The Generals look at each other. Nobody wants to give the dear leader bad news.

Finally General Ri stands up. "We will successfully launch twelve ICBM missiles in just over an hour. Then after launch, they should be hitting the American cities within thirty to forty minutes."

The dear leader sits and smiles. After forty years of delay and deceit, the North Korean leader is about to deal the West a shocking blow. His grandfather, his father and now he faced the Americans and the West and negotiated concessions and time. Now he has developed what his father could only dream of; a nuclear arsenal. He knows it will probably result in the loss of his country, but that was going to happen anyway. His only hope was to work with the Iranians and hit the Americans with all he has. If their assault fails, he is confident that the Chinese will take care of him and his family.

"Contact our Iranian brothers and let them know we are initiating our part of the bargain. Now they need to do the same."

The Generals know about the triad of power with Iran and al-Qaeda that Kim has cultivated over the past decade is now ready to act. This plan they believe will result in a world war and the overthrow of the western governments. Kim has read the papers about the racial discord in America, the college students rioting in the streets, police being shot in the major cities, ANTIFA radicals setting off bombs. America is coming apart by the seams. He intends to rip it apart and allow his partners to tear it down. It is a dangerous game that North Korea is playing, aligning themselves with the Iranians and in proxy with al-Qaeda, but the old saying that the enemy of my enemy is my friend, is true in this case. Kim Jong-Un smiles to himself. He will lead the biggest geo-political change in the past thousand years.

After the fall of America and Europe, he will be the one to unify Korea under his control.

Chapter 2

Washington DC
August 22nd

The President just arrived at the Situation Room when all hell broke loose.

President Baker's chief of staff rushes up to the President, eyes wide with panic. "It looks like Kim is going to launch his ICBMs."

The President looks to his Generals. "What the hell?"

General Seibert turns and salutes the commander-in-chief, "Sir, somehow Kim must have been tipped off. We need to move our forces into position for a counter-attack. There is no way he could have detected our troop build up and the positioning of our air assets. Someone

16

leaked our plan. We just detected the fueling of their ICBMs. They have also started positioning their troops along the DMZ."

"How the hell did he know? Can we hit his ICBMs before they are fueled?"

The General shakes his head. "No sir. We have just ten minutes until they are ready. Then it will be up to Kim to decide to launch. They may be just fueling to provoke a response from us or just to be ready. But personally I think he knows about our plans and has decided to launch first."

"Damn. Our military buildup was designed to put Kim in a box. Bring him to the table to negotiate more honestly. Now it looks like he has decided to start a war. If he launches, we need to hit him hard."

The President walks slowly around the room contemplating the situation. "Ok, continue with our plan. What about defensive systems if they do launch?"

General Seibert reaches over and picks up a folder and flips it open. "We have several dozen THAAD systems along the Alaska coast and northwestern U.S. ready to shoot them down. We also have THAAD systems in Japan and South Korea in the event that bastard shoots any birds in their direction."

The President knows that the THAAD system is the U.S. designed Terminal High Altitude Area Defense system designed to shoot down short, medium and ICBM ballistic missiles in their terminal phase of descent and re-entry by intercepting it with a hit-to-kill approach. The system has been promising, but it has only been tested on single incoming ICBMs. The President looks at the large monitor and sees the might of the United States military positioned for an attack on North

Korea, but now he worries that all that might could be for nothing if the North Korean ICBMs get through and destroy American cities.

Suddenly an Air Force Major tasked with monitoring the North Korean ICBMs yells, "Launching!"

All eyes turn to a satellite real-time feed over North Korea. The software shows a red circle rising from the surface, and then another, then another. Twelve in all.

"God-damn. General how long until they hit us?"

The General shakes his head. "We will have to determine the trajectory of each missile. That should take our software less than a minute, but probably 30-40 minutes depending on their targets. We have put all our THAAD systems on alert."

All around the situation room, every person seemed to be moving with determined purpose.

"We are sending out an alert to all communications centers telling all citizens to take shelter" says the communications officer. "We just went to DEFCON 1."

"Seven ICBMs are targeting the U.S. mainland. One ICBM is heading for Hawaii. Two ICBMs are heading for South Korea! Two for Japan!" Yells the Major.

The President watches the monitor and sees two missiles racing south towards Seoul, South Korea. "Six minutes to impact."

Suddenly they see two blue circles intercepting a pair of red triangles and they turn to green squares. "Got them both! The THAAD system shot down both missiles!"

Over Japan, the two missiles heading east are reaching their zenith. As the missiles begin their decent towards Japan, the THAAD system fires multiple defensive missiles. The President and all of the military staff watch as the missile tracks race towards each other. This is a tough mission, like shooting a bullet at another bullet. One trace of a THAAD missile slides by the North Korean ICBM, but then another THAAD intercepts and the software confirms the kill with a green square. A joyous yell goes up from all of the military personnel in the room. The second ICBM now is racing down its trajectory towards Tokyo. A THAAD missile trace moves toward the ICBM and then misses. A second THAAD missile is right behind the first. Just seconds behind. Everyone, including the President, is holding their breath. As they all watch, the ICBM and the THAAD missile traces intersect, but then the ICBM continues on its decent.

"Crap! Their ICBM is going to hit Tokyo."

"What about the eight aimed at us?"

"Sir, within the next fifteen minutes our THAAD systems will begin to shoot our defensive missiles. We are tracking the North Korean ICBMs up on the main screen. But three of the eight failed in launch."

All eyes in the room focus on the five red triangles moving slowly across a large map of the world, heading for the continental U.S. and Hawaii.

"Make sure there is an alert on all television and radio. Contact the FAA to ground all aircraft. Alert all military bases to go into lockdown."

As the ICBMs begin their descent, blue circles begin to rise up to meet them. Several miss, but the sheer number of THAAD missiles is impressive.

One after another, after another of the North Korean ICBMs are intercepted and the screen shows green squares signifying a hit. After just ten minutes it's all over.   All of the North Korean ICBMs aimed at the U.S. have been neutralized.

"Mr. President, we should get your family into the PEOC (Presidential Emergency Operations Center) just in case the North Koreans have more ICBMs."

The President grimly nods.   "Ok, but they just gave us the justification for an all out attack.   Launch the attack. Conventional arms only! Give'm hell boys!"

The President had tried to negotiate with Kim Jong-Un. It seemed to be going well until the Americans discovered a secret nuclear arsenal and ballistic missile program. When confronted, the North Koreans broke off talks and prepared for war.

After kissing the first lady, his wife, daughter and grandsons are led to safety under the White House in the secure bunker. Clare's husband and the other two of her children had been moved to Cheyenne Mountain where they will be safe from any

23

additional nuclear attack on Denver. Several of the President's top aides and multiple military leaders are all watching a large screen showing the detonation of multiple missiles that take out the remaining missile sites that had not yet been hit. Also shown are the B-52s, stealth bombers and stealth fighters taking out the NKPR military installations.

Kim had launched twelve ICBMs. This surprised the American military, but they were prepared. Once in the Situation Room, the President has been on the phone with the leaders of Britain, France, Germany, South Korea, India and other key leaders as well as Russia and China. Those last two phone calls were not pleasant. But the President was clear. The North Koreans fired eight nuclear-tipped ICBM missiles directly at the United States. The U.S. responded as any other country would at being attacked. Additionally Tokyo has been nuked.   Both China and Russia understand the use of power when provoked.

"Mr. Xi, we understand your concern about a unified Korea. Our military will try to negotiate a transition to peace, but Kim Jung-Un must step down and be tried for crimes against his people. If he is still alive, we would ask that China help with the cease fire after our troops have taken Pyongyang."

The President listens to the translation and the reply. He smiles.

"Yes Mr. General Secretary. We will keep you and your military appraised of our progress, but we expect no interference with our mission."

The President hangs up and lets out a long breath. "Well, at this point both the Russians and China are on the sidelines. Both, I believe, are relieved that Kim has been or will be taken out. But from their standpoint a nuclear Korean peninsula was very dangerous and they both know that Kim was a rabid dog."

The generals are busy directing the war and moving military assets towards North Korea. Even though the THAAD systems shot down the nuclear missiles, other conventional missiles did get through and caused considerable damage and killed thousands of civilians in South Korea. But several hours after the start of the war, the Americans and South Koreans have destroyed most of the military assets of the North. Unfortunately one of the nuclear missiles did get through and hit Tokyo. The world is shocked that Japan has suffered another nuclear attack, almost seventy-three years to the day after the Americans dropped a nuclear bomb on Nagasaki to end WWII. Current reports from Japan say that several hundred thousand Japanese were killed or injured from the North Korea attack.

Communications have been spotty at best, but the NSA and the CIA have continued to stream the latest information and data to the White House.

"Mr. President, we have confirmed that one NKPR ICBM missile did get through and hit just north of Tokyo."

The President shakes his head. "Damn. What about South Korea?"

"Nothing yet Sir. But it will be bad."

The President sits and considers this new information. "What about civilian casualties in Japan?"

The General is handed a piece of paper from his assistant. "From the nuclear attack directly? Too many died, probably several hundred thousand. Too early to tell. Before the ICBM exploded, they had almost five hundred commercial airliners in the air. Unfortunately because of the short distance

27

between North Korea and Japan, they had only ten minutes warning before the missile hit. Almost sixty airliners crashed. Some were coming in from overseas and couldn't get down, but several were just too far from airports that could accommodate them and they tried to put down on highways or in the sea. At this point with communications very limited, we have no idea how many people may have survived."

The President rises and walks over to a table with water and packaged snacks. "So what is the situation on the ground?"

The General clears his throat.

"The South Koreans have pounded the North Korean missile batteries and the troops just north of the DMZ. Of course some of the North Korean's missiles have gotten through and have hit Seoul and other cities.

"Well, thank God we were able to shoot down Kim's nukes.   I knew we couldn't trust him."

Suddenly an aide to the Joint Chiefs enters the Situation Room.   He hands the General a note.

After reading the note, the General turns to the group. "Mr. President, we have detected a launch of three ICBMs from Syria. We are attempting to bring them down, but we used most of our interceptor missiles to take down the North Korean initial launch. Our analysts believe they will get through."

The President stands up straighter. "Syria?   What the hell? "What are the targets?"

"Looking   at   the   altitude   and direction, our analysts believe they are targeting Western, Central and Eastern United States.

"Could this be Iran?"

The General shakes his head. "Could be Iran, could be Russia, or could be al-Qaeda."

"What about THAAD sites in Europe?"

"We can only hit the ICBMs during their re-entry. The missiles are coming in from an orbit that won't allow us to hit them until they get closer. We are alerting our THAAD systems on the eastern seaboard, but the ICBMs are coming in over Canada."

An Air Force staff sergeant turns from his terminal and yells. "The ICBMs are tracking to three targets in the U.S., that doesn't make sense."

"The Iranians probably moved Russian RT-12M2 missiles on portable launchers into Syria for deniability. They control the Southeastern quadrant with the Syrian government forces and working hand-in-hand with al-Qaeda and ISIL. The

30

three ICBMs were launched near Deir Az
Zor, in Eastern Syria" says the National
Security Advisor.

The General moves over and looks
at the monitor. "Damn. They are going to
detonate the ICBMs over the U.S., not hit us.
They are going to do a HEMP; a High
Altitude Electromagnetic Pulse."

The President reacts immediately.
"We have to warn the Congress, the
Supreme Court, the White House staff and
the American public!"

"Yes sir. A general warning on the
Emergency Warning System by FEMA has
been initiated. I will place calls to all
branches of the government, but unless
they get to a hardened site within thirty
minutes they will be exposed."

The President runs his hand through
his hair. "I want that area in Syria destroyed.
Every military force taken out. I don't care

if they are Iranian, Russia or Syrian. Then we'll deal with Iran."

General Seibert nods. "Yes sir! We have several drones in the area and they are tracking the launchers and the troops that were responsible. We have multiple assets available Qatar. They have been launched to take them out."

The Secretary of Defense speaks up. "I just heard from Israel, they have put their military on alert and would be available to hit Iran if we determine that the ICBMs are Iranian. They of course are also concerned that Iran will shoot a few nukes their way. But if they do that, Israel will destroy Iran with their own nuclear missiles."

"Mr. President, you should move into the PEOC along with the rest of the Joint Chiefs of Staff."

The President nods and leaves the Situation Room knowing he can follow the troop movements in the PEOC but wanting to be in the middle of the action.

In the PEOC, the President and the rest of his staff continue to watch the American attack unfold in North Korea while three nuclear missiles are streaking towards the American homeland.

Chapter 3

Los Angeles, CA
August 22nd

Jennifer Aldin happened to pick up her ex-husband's voice mail from his CIA jet over the Atlantic and acted quickly. She told her receptionist about the message and both women rushed to get home. But first Jennifer called her daughter Mary and told her to leave class immediately and get home, but didn't tell her why.

They both arrived at the same time; Mary sweaty from running the two miles from her school to her home. Mary rushes her daughter into their home while at the same time telling her about her father's phone call.

Placing blankets over the windows, the women try to insulate the house.

Jihadi White Christmas

Jennifer turns on the radio and the television to try to get any new information. The major channels have a warning of an imminent threat. Then suddenly the television and radio stop. There is dead silence in the house. Both Jennifer and Mary stand still looking at each other.

Jennifer has no idea what to expect. What this just a hoax? Did the nukes target another city, not L.A.?

"We need to prepare. I think we were hit with an Electro-Magnetic Pulse; an EMP.

Mary looks puzzled. "What is an EMP?"

Jennifer continues to cover the windows with blankets. "It is when a nuclear bomb is exploded above the Earth's surface, I think several hundred miles above and what it does is fry all the electronics in a wide area. I think that is why our television and radio stopped working."

Mary moves to the refrigerator and opens the door and grabs an orange juice.

"Close the door! We have to try to retain the cold in there as long as we can."

"Why?"

"There is no electricity, there will be no telephones, and no water!" Jennifer realizes that they have to store as much water as possible. "Get any large container and fill it with water."

"What about my cellular phone?" Mary says taking the iPhone out of her pocket.

"It won't work. No wireless communications, no communications at all. The whole telecommunication system is probably down."

Mary immediately starts pulling large pots from the cupboards. She turns on the faucets and gets a rush of water, then just a slow stream of water comes out. "Try the bathtub, see if you can fill it."

Mary races upstairs to the master bedroom and starts to run the water. It comes out slowly in a steady dribble. She then runs downstairs and sees her mom counting the canned goods and other food in the kitchen. "Luckily I just went to Costco yesterday. In the garage I have two cases of water."

"How long will the electricity be off?" Asks Mary.

Jennifer remembers talking with Mark about his EMP training as a SEAL. "I don't know honey, could be months."

Mary's face shows the shock of that statement. "Months?" She suddenly breaks down into tears. "What about school? I have a soccer game on Saturday!"

Jennifer comes to her daughter and pulls her into her arms. "I know honey, I am sorry. But we have to just survive until the government gets the electricity going and they can deliver food and water."

Jennifer knows they are fairly safe at the moment; but people who are not prepared, who don't have food or water will do anything to survive. Society will break down, lawlessness will take root. Jennifer shivers with the knowledge that the longer the blackout continues, the more dangerous it will become for them.

"What about the water in the pool?" Mary says.

Jennifer smiles. "I don't know. The water is chlorinated but maybe if we boil some, we will be able to drink it. Gather all the matches we have and we'll have to make a fire pit out back to boil our water and ...."

Suddenly there is a knock on her door. Jennifer freezes. "Stay here. I'll see who is there."

Jennifer walks to the door and looks through a side window and sees a neighbor standing on her door step.

She opens the door and smiles. "Hi Dominick, I guess it's a blackout."

Dominick is a neighbor from across the street. He is an investment banker and day trader. He is home most of the day and Jennifer always thought he was a creepy guy. He always seemed to be outside walking his dog while on his cellular phone when Jennifer would leave for her office. He would watch her come out of the house and yell a greeting or just smile, then watch her as she would enter her car and drive away.

"Our electricity is out, probably like yours I guess?" Dominick says.

He is a bit taller than Jennifer and probably 260 lbs. Too much alcohol, too much rich food and too little exercise over the past thirty years has resulted in an out-of-shape, entitled multi-millionaire.

"I think they should have it solved in a few hours. How is Abby?" Trying to distract Roger's gaze from Jennifer's chest.

His eyes drift upward. "Oh she is fine. Having her third bloodymary."

Suddenly his eyes move to beyond Jennifer. "Hey Mary, how are you? I would have thought you'd be in school."

Jennifer half turns and sees her daughter at her shoulder.

"Mom called and told me to come home."

Roger looks surprised. "Did you get an early warning about the blackout?" Looking at Jennifer.

"One of my patients works for Southern California Edison and told me about a potential overload", she lies. "I thought it would be best to be home if it happened."

Jennifer smiles weakly.

"Yeah, is Mark heading home?"

Jennifer freezes, the smile on his face is not neighborly.

"He should be home shortly."

"Well, we have solar battery so I might have some limited electricity. Come on over if you need anything." Dominick says with a wink and a smile.

Jennifer closes the door and locks it.

"God, what a creep." Says Mary.

"We can't let people know that your father is not here or that we got an advance warning. Everyone will figure it out within a day or two. At that point, it might be every person for themselves. We have to prepare for that."

Chapter 4

Belize
August 22nd

The Air Force pilots maneuver the CIA jet towards the Belize City International Airport after getting word that North Korea was shooting ICBMs at the United States. The plane is cleared for landing and swoops onto the 9700 foot runway. After landing and roll out, the jet taxis to a private hanger that the pilot arranged for after the change in destinations.

Mark and Michelle disembark after talking with the Air Force officers. The jet has onboard a small arsenal of weapons including four M16A rifles, six Beretta M9 pistols, two XM2010 Enhanced Sniper rifles, two XM 25 Counter Defilade Target Engagement Systems and a box of grenades. They discuss the protection of the jet.

"We will refuel while we can and we've rented this private hanger for two weeks, we can extend as we need to." Says the pilot.

Mark nods, "Ok, great. One of you should stay with the jet at all times. The other doing a perimeter patrol varying the time. Each of you should be armed and use deadly force if required to protect the jet. We'll take over when we get back."

Michelle jumps in. "I'll contact the Belize military and see if they will assign a few of their men as an extra level of protection. We'll head to the U.S. embassy and try to get more information on what is happening back home, the extent of the damage and what our next steps are."

The two pilots nod affirmatively and one directs over a fuel truck to refill the tanks and begin his maintenance review.

The other goes inside the jet to get his M16A rife and a side arm.

Mark and Michelle walk into the terminal and look for a car rental site. As they walk down one hallway, Michelle sees a television in one of the bars showing a photo of Washington D.C. and several commentators speaking.

"Let's check this out." Motioning towards the television, they see that it's a BBC broadcast.

They move into the bar and ask the bartender to turn up the sound. After he does, they hear one of the commentators saying; "... the United States attack on North Korea has been for the most part very successful. Over eighty percent of the North Korea military capability has been destroyed as reported by Reuters. It is reported that North Korea fired a dozen missiles first at the United States, and then

President Baker responded with overpowering force."

Another commentator breaks in. "It seems that the NKPR fired those missiles in response to the United States moving military assets towards North Korea. They were justified."

"Justified? The United States moves military assets around the world on a regular basis, it looks like Kim Jong-Un feared an American attack and reacted first." Says the other commentator.

The moderator takes over. "To bring everyone up to speed; The United States and North Korea went to war this morning. The information we have at this point shows that North Korea fired a dozen ICBM missiles, eight at the United States, two at South Korea and two at Japan. All of those missiles shot at the U.S. were shot down by the U.S. missile defense system, but one of the missiles reached their target in Japan. Just coming in; Breaking News! Our latest information from the Canadian government says that three missiles were detonated two hundred miles above continental U.S. with one over the state of Colorado, one over the state of Iowa and the third over Northern Virginia."

The moderator takes a deep breath and looks directly into the camera. "At that point, all communications from the United States has ceased. These were EMP blasts that would impact most electronic devices including cellular phones, car electrical systems, airplane systems, and the United States electrical grid and of course it's telecommunication systems."

One of the commentators starts to describe Electromagnetic Pulse devices and how they work and the damage they can do.

At this point Michelle and Mark leave the bar to find a vehicle.

Jihadi White Christmas

"Damn, this could be really bad. I was briefed on EMP attacks and the aftermath, it's not good. First the public will stay calm for a few days waiting for the Federal government to turn on the lights. The food supply will be consumed within a week. Because the trucks that bring food to stores stop, there will be no resupply. Within days there will be riots in the major cities; New York, Chicago, Los Angeles, San Francisco, Atlanta and others will collapse into total chaos."

They take an escalator down one level and spot the car rental companies.

"The medical system will breakdown, disease and societal collapse will kill millions. The study I saw was that within a year unless the government can restore order and electrical power, the United States population will drop by 80-90 percent."

Mark can't believe what he is hearing, but he knows Michelle understands what she is talking about.

"We need to get to the embassy as soon as possible and try to establish a connection with the White House. Hopefully the President and his family are safe."

Chapter 5

Tehran Iran
August 23rd

The leadership of the Iranian Mullahs has gathered along with General Aziz the head of the Revolutionary Guards. After the decision was made to move the Russian ICBMs into Syria, General Aziz knew it was only a matter of time before either the Israelis or the Americans spotted them. The Mullahs didn't want to attack America unless there was no other choice. But now that their gambit of releasing the Red Death virus upon the world was stopped, the European Union, the Americans and even the Russians and Chinese are against them. All are calling for a regime change and an end to the radical Islamic ideology in Iran. They are pushing a government much like

Turkey that has both Muslims and non-Muslims ruling the country.

The theocracy guided by the radical Islamic ideology has ruled Iran for the past forty years. The supreme leader and the clerics will not have their power usurped by the West. After receiving the $1.2 Billion dollar payment from the United States for the nuclear deal in 2015, the military was upgraded and now they believe they are capable to destroying Israel.

Of course the agreement was suppose to stop the Iranian nuclear program, but Iran had built a totally secret underground facility that continued the development of both a nuclear warheads and ballistic missiles to deliver them to anywhere in the world. But the most important part of the agreement was the lifting of the sanctions. Those sanctions were strangling the Iranian economy. They were not able to sell oil and therefore could not buy much needed food, medicine and other basics to keep the Iranian population pacified. The nuclear agreement happened just in time. There were millions of Iranians that were getting ready to revolt. But with the sanctions lifted, it was like taking the top off a tea kettle just before it blew. Now the Iranians are reaping almost $1 Billion dollars per month from oil exports, more than enough to fund their economy and export terror to the West.

General Aziz stands before the supreme leader and the Mullahs and informs them of their progress. "As you know, we moved three Russian RT-12M2 missiles with 5 KT nuclear warheads to Southeastern Syria four weeks ago when the Red Death virus attack was stopped. The West in coordination with Russia and China are planning devastating sanctions like we've never seen. It will lead to our countries' demise. We had to act. So at 3 am this morning, we launched the three nuclear missiles at the United States designed to explode two hundred miles above the U.S. causing an EMP event that will knock out every electrical device in the country. This will decimate America, the country will fall into riots but at the same time North Korea has launched twelve of their nuclear ICBMs at the United States, South Korea and Japan. I believe we will be successful in causing a third world war from which the Muslim people, more specifically Iran will emerge victorious."

There are rumblings among the Mullahs, but General Aziz continues. "The ICBMs were launched from Syria and no doubt the Americans know that, but they don't know if it was us, the Russians or our brothers in al-Qaeda. That indecision is all we need to be successful."

The supreme leader slowly rises from his seat. He is an old man and knows his time to rule is short. "My brothers, we are at a crossroads in the history of our great country. This is our time to rule. It is our destiny from Allah. Allah 'arbar! Allah 'arbar! Allah 'arbar!"

All of Mullahs and the military present including General Aziz chant the famous God is Greater slogan. Aziz is not that religious, just power hungry. He wants the military to rule Iran and all of the Middle East. If Iran can survive this crisis, then he plans another revolution one in which his Revolutionary Guards will take power and he, General Aziz and his son will rule Iran and most of the Middle East will an iron fist.

Chapter 6

Washington D.C.
August 23rd

The majority of Congress and the Senate were rushed into the basement of the Capital Building. They were in session when the North Koreans launched their surprise attack. There wasn't time to get the political leadership to either the Greenbrier Resort and Bunker in White Sulphur Springs, WVa or to Raven Rock in Pennsylvania. Both had been built to house the Congress in the event of a nuclear war. Of course everyone thought they would have a slow build up to a war and have time to travel to one of these sites before the missiles hit. They made a critical mistake.

Jihadi White Christmas

The Speaker of the House and the President Pro Tempore of the Senate are on opposite sides of the political spectrum and have had many arguments about policy over the past thirty years in politics. One represents the Republicans, the other the Democrats. But the issue is that the President ran as an independent and surprisingly won. So neither of these men got the power they craved.

Now they are together, crowded into the basement of the Capitol Building. During a session focused on a bill to increase sanctions on Iran for its recent provocations; suddenly the Capitol police entered the House chamber and hustled the Congress members to the basement, while the public was led to the exits. The Senate chamber is similarly emptied and moved to the same basement area below the two seats of power.

The Speaker of the House is on his cellular phone with his chief of staff. "Margie, what is happening?"

Several members are crowded around the Speaker trying to listen to his conversation.

"Oh my God, they launched missiles?"

There is a murmur of alarm.

The Speaker tells his chief of staff on the phone; "Ok, get to a safe place. The basement. Good luck Margie. God bless you."

He hangs up and turns to the gathered Congress people. "The North Koreans launched missiles at us. Our military will try to shoot them down, but if they miss we could be hit in about thirty minutes."

Suddenly all of the members get on their phones to call their families. Some families are in their home states, some are in Washington D.C., but all are threatened as are three hundred thirty million Americans. After a few minutes of each member of the Congress trying to get information, they realize that the United States is at war with North Korea.

"How the hell could President Baker do this? He has to get approval from us for a shooting war!"

Other members of Congress argue that if Kim Jong-Un fired first, then the President has the authority and indeed the responsibility to protect the United States. The arguments continue back and forth.

Suddenly one of the Senators, then another get calls saying that the THAAD systems were able to hit each of the ICBMs targeting the U.S. There is a cheer and all of the Senators and Congress people start towards the exit.

There are several Capitol police guarding the doors to the basement. When one of the Senators tries to exit the basement he is stopped.

"I am a United States Senator, I demand that I be allowed to leave!"

Suddenly all of the cellular phones stop working. The panic of their communications to the outside being cut off is the trigger.

Several other Senators and Congress people also begin to yell. But the guards hold their ground. Suddenly, one of the Senators grabs the guard's gun and several Congressmen push the other guard to the ground.

"Stop, it's for our protection that we are down here!" Yells the Speaker. But the panic has overtaken the crowd. Most of the people rush out of the basement.

The Speaker shakes his head.

"Damn fools. Obviously Washington D.C. was not hit, but the communications system has probably been overwhelmed.

Jihadi White Christmas

We should just wait for the military to take control and then we can sort it out."

While the leadership waits, three Syrian missiles are hitting their apogee and starting it's re-entry towards America. Life in the United States of America is about to change dramatically.

Chapter 7

NORAD, Colorado Springs, CO
August 23rd

The NORAD commanders detected the Syrian launch and immediately contacted their missile defense system. Unfortunately, most of the defensive missiles, which were launched to try to stop the twelve ICBMs in the initial attack on South Korea, Japan and America are now useless.

The NORAD commanding General Greg Scott is pacing back and forth in front of the large screen showing all of the American military assets in the war theatre.

"How did we miss that launch site? The CIA told us that the Iran had ICBMs, but not with nukes. We have to assume these missiles are nuclear armed," Shouts the Air Force General. "What assets do we have to shoot it down?"

Major Whitehead steps forward, "During the first and second stages, we have very little chance at this point to intercept it. During the third stage after it reaches its apogee, we have several missiles ready to launch from Europe. If we miss, then we'll have another chance as it does it's re-entry from its suborbital trajectory."

The General nods. He knows all this. "What are the targets?"

The major hits several keystrokes on his computer keyboard. Suddenly a trajectory shows how the missiles will travel and their final destinations. "If the ICBMs are programmed for an EMP, they should detonate within the next ten minutes. If they are programmed for a ground burst, then they will detonate over Washington

D.C., Omaha NE and Denver, CO in sixteen minutes."

"God help them." The Major says still looking at the screen. "We have one Terminal High Altitude Area Defense (THAAD) System available in Poland. They are targeting the ICBMs now."

The General and the staff see the THAAD system missiles represented by red triangles moving slowly at first from the launch point. At the same time the system shows the THAAD missiles arching from the East Coast of the United States towards the ICBMs now over northern Canada.

One of the THAAD missiles trajectory continues to track towards the ICBM.

"One minute to impact."

The collective command is silent, all watching the screen.

"Thirty seconds to impact. Ten, nine, eight, seven, six, five, four, three..."

Then the group sees the THAAD missile track move past the ICBM.

"Missed.   Second THAAD missile closing. Impact is twenty seconds."

Everyone in the room is holding their breath knowing that another miss will result in hundreds of thousands of Americans dead.

"Ten, nine, eight, seven, six, five, four, three..."

The THAAD missile streaks toward the ICBM. It's like two bullets approaching each other at 6-7 Km per second. Just a slight miscalculation and they will pass by each other.

The General and others watch as the tracks cross, and then continue.   Another miss.

"Damn. Are there any Aegis Missile systems in the area?"

The Major types in some additional keystrokes, "No sir. Closest Aegis Ballistic system is off the coast of North Carolina, too far to be effective."

"Ok, alert the National Military Command Center at the Pentagon. Let them know that three suspected nuclear devices may impact the Washington D.C., Kansas and Denver areas in approximately sixteen minutes."

The NORAD staff watches helplessly as the Syrian ICBMs continue their path to death and destruction. After five minutes, the three Iranian ICBMs detonate high over the United State of America.

Chapter 8

Washington D.C.
August 23rd

The President is sitting in the Situation Room watching the same screen from NORAD. As the second missile misses, he drops his head into his hands.

"Damn."

"Sir, we should prepare for the impact. The facility is rated to be able to survive a nuclear attack, but there will be damage. We should move now to the containment area."

The President rises and wearily follows the General out of the Situation Room and down a long hallway to the Presidential Emergency Operations Center. Two marine guards stand at attention at the PEOC vault doors. Inside are the

President's wife, his daughter Clare and his two grandchildren. They run to the President and his arms envelope them.

Also inside are the Joint Chiefs of Staff, the National Security Advisor and several of the other President's staff. The Vice President and his staff have been flown to Peters Mountain in Virginia the Intelligence Agencies' secure bunker.

As the countdown comes to the final minute, the President gathers his family together and they all hold hands and wait.

Everyone sits quietly, waiting for the blast. But there is only silence. After a minute, one of the secure phones rings and everyone jumps.

The National Security Advisor answers the phone and hands it to the President.

"Yes Fred, we are ok. What about you? Good, Good. When you get some idea of the damage, let me know. Thanks."

Jihadi White Christmas

The President looks around the room. "The Vice President, his family and his staff are safe. The CIA personnel at Peters Mountain are operational and gathering data on the attack on the Capitol and also how things are going in North Korea. The three ICBMs were EMP blasts."

General Seibert is closely watching another screen. "Our troops are crossing the DMZ and meeting some resistance. Armor and the marines should be in P'yongyang within twelve hours. Its 121 miles as the crow flies, but probably 200 miles along their highway system."

The President now focuses on the war with North Korea. "What about Kim Jong-Un?"

The General pulls up a secure email from his second-in-command in South Korea. "We hit the Presidential palace with three bunker busters. If Kim was there, he is definitely dead. However, they obviously got a tip so I would assume he moved. We are monitoring their military communications and if we hear that he is still alive, then we'll try to track him down."

The President walks around his desk. "The biggest issue is the American public. With the EMPs, the electrical grid will be down, most transportation will be stopped and food will become scarce. I think we need to start moving the military and National Guard out into the major cities to prevent rioting and looting."

The National Security Advisor, Debra Rodriguez steps forward. "Mr. President, we can have troops on the streets within twelve hours. That will slow down the rioting, but without food and water even an army of troops will not stop people from a full scaled riot."

"What about the national food reserve? Can we use some of that to get food to distribution points around the country?" asks the President.

"The issue is transportation; we don't know yet how bad the electronics were fried due to the EMPs. Older models that don't have the latest electronics might still work or can be repaired. But we do have several thousand military vehicles in various hardened facilities that probably survived and could be used to transport food and water. We could set up a shipping network until the electrical grid can be fixed and brought back to operational status," Says Debra Rodriguez.

"Ok, move key military assets to the major cities and get those military vehicles to bring food and water where it's needed. Also, get the National Guard out now if possible," says the President.

"Also get the military to send a few people to contact and bring the electrical and communications company leaders to the White House where they can put together a plan to repair the electrical and communications grids. That has to be a priority. Without electricity and communications, the American public may panic. We have to reassure them, let them know the American government is working on their behalf and let them know what has happened."

The phone rings again. "Mr. President, its Michelle Samaha."

The President picks up the phone. "Michelle, how are you?"

"We are safe Mr. President. We diverted to Belize."

"In Belize? Excellent. Yes, we are ok currently. That bastard Kim tried to nuke Washington DC. The biggest issue is that the Iranians exploded three ICBMs over the United States causing EMP damage throughout the country. It's going to be a hell of a mess. Also Tokyo was hit with a nuke, thousands killed there."

Michelle replies, "Yes Mr. President we saw the report on a European TV show. Is there anything we can do?"

The President pauses for a few seconds, then answers. "We are unsure if we killed Kim. He was tipped off and the Generals are sure he moved from his Presidential Palace prior to our attack. The marines should be in P'yongyang within the next twenty-four hours and will at that point start a search for him. But what I'd like you and Mark to think about working on is a plan to punish Iran. I'd like perhaps that you and Mark could aid in that effort?"

"Mr. President, we will do whatever is needed."

"Ok Michelle. I am happy you and Mark are safe. Come up with a plan and get back to me as soon as you can. Ok, Good bye."

Chapter 9

Belize

August 23rd

Michelle hangs up the phone and turns to Mark. "The President is safe as are Clare and the boys. Kim tried to nuke the United States, but failed. Unfortunately Tokyo was hit. South Korea and the U.S. military have begun the assault on North Korea. However, they believe that Iran launched three ICBMs from Syria which exploded over the U.S. and caused massive EMP damages."

Mark swears softly. "Damn, what about China and Russia?"

"I think they are sitting on the sidelines, for now. Our nuclear arsenal is still intact and operational and they know we would respond if they tried anything.

But I wouldn't be surprised if China gets involved in the North Korea war. They will not want a unified Korea on their doorstep."

Michelle and Mark are in the U.S. Embassy SKIF and they know their conversations are secure.

"When are we going back?" asks Mark.

"The President wants us to come up with a plan to punish Iran for their actions. We'll have to get back to S-Cubed as soon as we can."

Mark picks up the secure phone and dials his ex-wife's home phone. "I know this is a long shot, but I hope I can get through to Jennifer and Mary and see if they are safe." Mark finishes dialing, but hears nothing. Then a voice saying that "That number is not available at this time." Mark hangs up and shakes his head. "No luck there."

Mark starts to head for the door. "With the EMP damage, it will be interesting to land in the Washington D.C. area and get to the office."

Michelle following him says. "We should try to get in touch with the S-Cubed staff and see if their equipment is still operational, and let them know where we are."

They exit the SKIF and meet with the Ambassador and her assistant. They inform her that the President and Vice President are safe and that the United States government is functional. Also that North Korea tried to nuke Washington D.C. but that attack was stopped, but that three ICBMs from Syria were launched and exploded over the U.S. and have caused massive EMP damage. The Ambassador is shocked.

"We may have to stay in Belize for several weeks until we know what is happening in the U.S. and the status of the war with North Korea." Michelle tells the Ambassador.

"We will give you any support you might need. The Belize government has been an excellent partner with the U.S."

Michelle smiles. "Thank you Ambassador. We have refueled our jet and have it staged in a private hanger. We'll provide our own security."

The Ambassador nods. "The only issue to be aware of is that Belize has a growing gang problem. MS-13 has started infiltrated Belize from El Salvador. If they find out about your jet, they would love to get an asset like that."

Michelle knows the MS-13 organization well. She knows that Mara Salvatrucha better known as MS, is a criminal gang originally from El Salvador that recruits young Latin American youths who become involved in drug distribution, child prostitution, abduction, robbery and murder. They are absolutely brutal and a growing cancer on the fabric of America. There are also indications that MS-13 has been talking with al-Qaeda about terrorism within the United States.

"What is the 13 for?" Asked Mark.

The gang has a ritual for new aspirants to join the gang called the *beat-in* for thirteen seconds. Therefore the MS-13 was born."

"Ok, we'll keep our eyes and ears open. Can we count on the Belize police?"

The Ambassador nods, "Yes, but they don't have the numbers to be too much help in case of an attack on you."

Michelle smiles. "Well, we have an arsenal that might surprise MS-13, if they do bother us."

With that, they all stand and Michelle and Mark thank the Ambassador for her help.

"We will be back every few days to talk with the President and have to establish communications with our offices and then start our planning for our return to the United States."

Michelle and Mark return to their car and drive out of the Embassy.

A young man kneeling on the opposite corner feeding a stray dog notes the license number. After the car drives away, he kicks the dog away and places a call describing the car and the two people inside, then hops on his motorcycle to follow them.

Chapter 10

Anju, North Korea
August 23rd

Kim Jong-Un is watching a monitor that shows the missile tracks for his twelve ICBMs aimed at South Korea, Japan and the United States. His Generals are watching also with apprehension. If the missiles are shot down or fail, then their leader will explode with anger. But they know they will not fail.

The Americans have pushed Kim into a corner. The negotiations with the South and the Americans went according to the script until the Americans insisted on spot inspections of not only their nuclear facilities but their conventional military sites. This was totally unacceptable to Kim. Over the years Kim Jong-Un learned from his

Jihadi White Christmas

Iranian brothers; concede minor points, promise to stop nuclear development, but hide the real nuclear program. The Iranians have been doing that for the past decade. Kim knows their nuclear warhead program is ready. He also knows that the Iranian ballistic missile program is ahead of his. Both sides have been sharing data and scientists for years. Now both countries are ready to exact their revenge and dominate their geopolitical regions and ignite a world war. Muslims will rise up in American and Europe, they can not lose.

The plan between the two countries is to disable the United States of America with EMPs and then Iran will take out Israel, Saudi Arabia and control the Middle East and North Korea will overrun South Korea and then invade Japan.

Kim knows the Americans will still be dangerous; but with the EMPs detonating over America, the military and the leadership will have to focus on their people, their cities and repairing their infrastructure.

"When will our missiles hit America?" The Chairman says not taking his eyes off the screen.

General Ri clears his throat. "We estimate another ten minutes. The missiles are starting their descent."

While they watch, the missiles heading for America begin to streak towards their targets. Kim shakes his head. "Where are their defensive missiles? Did we catch them totally unaware?"

The two generals glance at each other, and then General Ri speaks. "Yes, I believe the Americans are paper tigers. Their defensive systems haven't even responded."

Both Generals know the system has been rigged to not show defensive missiles. Their systems can't pick up opposing objects since the North Koreans do not have access to satellite data once promised by the Chinese. But they can't admit that to their leader. This is like a video game, rigged to show the North Korean missiles exploding on the American soil.

They all watch as their missiles streak towards South Korea, Japan, Hawaii and America. Within minutes it is clear to the Generals that the two missiles aimed at Seoul and Dongducheon the home to Camp Casey were shot down by the American THAAD system but the Dear Leader doesn't notice. He is watching the missile tracks on the main screen heading toward the United States. "How long until the missiles hit the U.S.?"

The Generals consult their notes. "Within the next eight minutes."

Suddenly there are yells from the console operators. One of the missiles has hit Tokyo.

General Gim Chi-Sung smiles. "Dear Leader, we have struck the Japanese. Tokyo is now a radioactive wasteland."

"General, the South Koreans and Americans have begun their assault. They have begun shelling the DMZ and most of our military sites. Our army is gathering ready for a counter-attack."

Kim Jong-Un nods. "Excellent."

The General Ri knows this is the end of their country and their rule over the people of North Korea. He believes that after the Americans defeat a foe, they step in with money to rebuild. They did that in WWII and he hopes the same will be done for his country. Once the war was started there is no hope that the North Korea army could defeat the South Koreans and Americans. He secretly hopes all of the ICBM missiles will either fail in their flight or be shot down. But now Tokyo has been destroyed. It was a beautiful city. General

Jihadi White Christmas

Ri went to Japan once for a secret meeting with the Americans a dozen years ago. But that was at the beginning of Kim Jong-Un rule and he was unwilling to truly negotiate for a peaceful end to the Korean War. Recently the Americans tried again in an effort to eliminate the North Korean nuclear program. But Kim Jong-Un had learned from the Iranians and what happened to Muammar Gaddafi in Libya. If a dictator loses power, he dies. Kim appeared to work with the Americans and the South Koreans while at the same time hiding his real nuclear program and his working closely with Iran. The Iranians had given him the ICBM technology and the software necessary for the system to work. In return, Kim had given the Iranians his nuclear bomb technology. It was a fair trade and a good partnership. Now both countries would attack their common enemy, America.

Chapter 11

Belize

August 23rd

Michelle has been listening to the BBC radio trying to understand the situation in the United States and in the Far East, as Mark and one of the pilots went out to get some food for dinner.

Michelle had arranged for the Belize military to station a jeep and three army regulars at the front of the hanger. It announces their presence but she figures MS-13 or whoever might want to steal the jet would already know about them being there. It was another layer of security.

Mark and the co-pilot have been gone for almost an hour and Michelle is starting to get worried. Suddenly the side door opens and Michelle reaches for her

M16A rifle and brings it to bear on the two forms. But then she lowers the weapon. Mark and the co-pilot enter holding multiple bags of food.

"Dinner, breakfast and lunch!" says Mark with a big smile. He brings the bags to a large table that has been set up on the other side of the jet.

Michelle smiles. Mark has kept his sense of humor even in this difficult time. "Chinese or Mexican?" Asks Michelle.

"Belizean. I got some rice and beans with chicken or shrimp cooked in coconut milk." Says Mark. "Plus I got some Johnny cakes."

Michelle starts unpacking the food. "Johnny cakes?"

Mark smiles. "Yeah, they are a specialty of Belize, a small baked bread cakes, plus some potato salad."

Everyone digs in and sits around the table eating and talking about the attack on the U.S. and the potential damage.

"What do you think has happened in the U.S. after an EMP attack?"

Michelle has been briefed on several scenarios, but believes the normalization of life in the United States could take one to two years.   Both pilots are Air Force and cleared for top secret discussions.   "The large cities will be hit hardest.   A lack of food and water will happen within a week or two, electricity out for a month or more, no transportation due to the EMP frying the electronics, no communications, no internet, some radio but no television. An increase in lawlessness,   rioting,   arson...   I   think however that the U.S. military will take over general policing activities to keep things under control."

Mark shakes his head.   "As I understand it, the three ICBMs were launched from Syria. Do you think they came from Iran?"

Michelle swallows a bite of the shrimp rice and beans. "I think so. They probably wanted to launch from there to have some deniability, but for sure the Iranians are behind this."

"Damn, I should have taken out General Aziz when I was there."

Michelle nods, then smiles. "That assassination would have been significantly more difficult. I am sure he has Revolutionary Guards all around him at all times. But maybe it's something we could suggest to the POTUS once things get more back to normal."

Mark takes a bite of one of the Johnny cakes. "Wow, this is really good! Try it with honey on it." With his mouth partially full, "Have you been able to connect with Ducky, Jonathan Bardsley or Kelly Campos?"

Michelle nods, "The S-Cubed site is totally secure and had been hardened just in the event of an EMP blast, as are many of the military sites. So I am confident they and everyone in that building are ok. But Ducky hadn't come in so they don't know where he is. We have stored food and water in the basement to keep a hundred people safe and fed for five years, so if we can get there or set up communications with them, then we'll be able to coordinate any plans the President has for us."

Mark and the pilots smile.

"I hope we can get back there as soon as possible, and then take out the bad guys, especially those Iranian bastards."

Just then there is an explosion just outside the hanger. Mark and Michelle grab their M16s and the pilots sprint to the jet to secure it and grab their weapons.

Jihadi White Christmas

As Mark hits the side door a hail of
bullets rake the side of the hanger and they
know they are in the fight of their lives.

Chapter 12

Tehran, Iran
August 23rd

General Aziz is confident that the Americans will not respond with nuclear weapons to the EMP attack on it's shores. From Canadian broadcasts, it seems the nuclear missiles fired from Syria did their job to cripple the United States of America. Over the past three months, a secret Revolutionary Guard unit disassembled, transported and reassembled the three nuclear ICBM missiles in Syria. All without the Americans or the Israelis prying eyes knowing what they were doing. This operation was initiated even while the Red Death virus was underway. It was an insurance policy against Israel not totally being infected by the Iranian hybrid virus.

The plan was to finish Israel off once the virus had decimated the Israeli military. But then the North Koreans who were suppose to launch eight ICBMs and devastate America, failed. The Iranian air force tapping into the Russian satellites to detect if the North Korean missiles hit the Great Satan, saw that the THAAD systems destroyed each ICBM or the missiles failed in flight. Unfortunately the Americans were able to shoot down most of the North Korean ICBMs, except for one missile that got through and hit Tokyo.

At that point, the Mullahs after consulting with the supreme leader decided to redirect their three ICBMs at the U.S. rather than Israel knowing that if they shot at Tel Aviv, the Israelis would destroy Iran with their nuclear arsenal. However, the Americans would foolishly have to verify that it was the Iranians that shot the missiles. That is one of the reasons the missiles were moved to Syria. It gave Iran deniability. Behind the scenes, they have instituted a disinformation campaign to blame al-Qaeda. The Americans will know the missiles were Russian, but not who launched them.

General Aziz enters the Revolutionary Guard headquarters and is saluted by the two guards at the door. Walking down a hall and up an elevator to his office, the General has called his direct reports to get a report on their progress. Entering his conference room, the General sees the six men that control the Revolutionary Guard and most of the military within Iran. They rise as he enters the conference room.

"Please be seated. Major General Jafari, would you give us report on the Quds Force deployment and actions?"

The Major General stands. "Gentlemen, the Quds Force has been on alert since the launch against the Americans. Our technical officers were able to redirect the ICBMs from Israel to America. The three missiles were reprogrammed to ignite at two hundred miles over the surface, spaced to affect the west, central and eastern regions of the country. The blasts will create an Electro-Magnetic Pulse. As you all know, this pulse fries any and all exposed electronics. The Americans are the most technologically advanced country in the world. But now they have just been thrust back to the 1950s."

All of the military leaders clap.

Jafari continues. "However, we have to remember that the United States military is still very deadly. Their nuclear force is of course, still operational. But we do not believe America will attack us with nuclear weapons. They are committed to non-nuclear wars, but the Islamic Republic of Iran does not play be the same rules."

He says with a smile. "The infidels must be defeated. The first step is to cripple the Great Satan. Make them look internally. Make their government focus on saving their people, not adventurism in the Middle East. Without the Americans in our backyard we can conquer Iraq, then Syria, then we will turn on Saudi Arabia, Oman, Qatar and finally the rest of the Middle East until the Persian Empire rises again to our rightful place."

All of the military leaders rise as one shouting and cheering. General Aziz smiles. He knows that this is a dangerous game. If the Americans can survive the EMP blast and repair their economy, then the Iranian plan will fail. But he believes the American society is soft. Too much television, too much food, too much technology, too much social media and too little discipline has made the Americans vulnerable to attack. They are a divided nation. The major powers won't come to their aid. Russia and China will scoop up the remnants of the U.S. economy. Europe will silently cheer that America has been taken down a peg and try to benefit from their weakness.

General Aziz stands and the group quiets. "We have accomplished a lot, but there is still a lot to do. Israel is our greatest enemy and must be destroyed. As we take more and more territory, we will tighten the noose around Israel. Our nuclear program is producing nuclear weapons at an astonishing pace. At some point, we will be able to match Israel's nuclear capabilities. Then we will be on equal footing and able to surround their country and squeeze like a boa constructor does with its prey. We must not fail! However, we can not underestimate America. They must be destroyed!"

Chapter 13

Washington D.C.
August 24th

After the attack on the United States, the President and his staff are trying to coordinate the U.S. military to repair the electrical grid, to distribute food and water to the major population centers and to restore order.

The major cities quickly dissolved into riots and death. Gangs and roving groups are preying on citizens who are at their mercy. Those with weapons are able to defend themselves, but many are robbed and killed for as little as a loaf of bread.

New York City, Chicago, Atlanta, Dallas, Los Angeles, St Louis and Houston have been particularly hard hit. Tens of thousands have died, millions displaced. The President listens intently, frowning.

"So what are we doing?" Asks the President.

The Homeland Security Secretary, Tom Johnson pauses from his report and looks up. "Mr. President, we are moving as many military assets into place as quickly as we can. Fortunately we have tens of thousands of military vehicles in hardened sites and they are being used to transport material and military personnel to key staging points."

The President rises and walks around the Situation Room located under the White House. "How quickly can we get the electrical grid operational? What about communications?"

General Seibert looks up. "Mr. President, we have activated the National Guard. They are being deployed into the major cities to help the police, to arrest looters and restore the rule of law. The military is working with the electrical companies to restore power and they are also leading food and water convoys to distribution centers. We should have our network established within the next week and I believe we will see a noticeable reduction in riots."

"God, I hope so. The key is getting the electrical grid up and running. Once that has happened, we can communicate via the radio and television. Reassure people that the Federal government is still in business, fixing the grid and restoring the peace."

In the Situation Room there is constant activity. Reports are coming in from military units around the country, describing what is happening in the major cities and the small towns. Major Wilcox has been collecting and collating the data from hundreds of military unit commanders who are reporting daily on what is happening in their area. He pulls together all of his notes and walks down a hallway to the Presidential Conference Room.

The President and his Joint Chiefs of Staff and multiple advisors are watching several large monitors as Major Simmons enters. He stands at attention waiting to be acknowledged. General Seibert sees him and salutes. "General, I have the latest report from our commanders in each of the six regions."

General Seibert and the President both give the Major their full attention. "Go ahead son."

The Major refers to his notes. "In the western region Los Angeles is still having riots and the gangs are controlling certain parts of the city. We are moving a combat regiment of fifteen hundred troops there to quell the riots." He looks down and continues. "Things are calming down in

Phoenix, Dallas and Denver. The smaller cities in the West are starting to get some of the water and food the National Guard is bringing in. If we can get the electrical grid operational, then we should be ok in the west."

The President nods, "What about the hot spots in the rest of the country?"

The Major flips his notes over and continues. "St Louis is a big issue, as are Chicago, Detroit, New York and Baltimore. Those cities have been ravaged by riots and arson. Thousands have been killed. We brought in the National Guard, but it's street to street fighting in some areas."

The President turns to his Homeland Security Secretary. "What about food and water to those areas? What is the latest on the electrical grid?

Tom Johnson looks up from his notes. "We have caravans using military trucks and a National Guard escort heading to each of those cities. The main threats are from gangs, especially MS-13. They are organized and hijacked a previous caravan to steal the food and the weapons. Twelve National Guard personnel were killed or wounded. Unfortunately this is happening around the country."

The President breaks in. "It's almost September, within two months it will get bitterly cold in the northern part of the country and then millions will die if we can't get the electrical grid up and running. That should be the number one priority."

General Seibert agrees. "Yes sir, we are throwing as many personnel as we can at the problem, while at the same time trying to restore peace. The electrical companies believe we can get the electrical grid mostly operational within sixty days."

"Damn, we need to accelerate those fixes. Get electricity flowing to the major cities! The smaller cities and in the countryside, those people are more self-reliant and should be able to weather this crisis on their own or with minimal support. But the big cities are potential flash points."

The President's Chief of Staff pipes up. "Mr. President, we need to get you on a national radio address to the American people and to the world. Let them know what happened, who is responsible and that America is still standing strong and will bring those who did this to justice. Those with hand crank radios or solar powered radios would get the message. Plus the CB community will spread the word. Then hopefully by word of mouth, the message will get out."

The President nods. "Ok, set it up and I'll write up a statement."

Chapter 14

Belize - August 24th

After a brief firefight, the MS-13 gang melted back into the jungle. It was now almost 1 am and Michelle spoke with the Belizean military officers who rushed to help their guards to fight off the attackers.

"Thank you for sending more fighters. We were within minutes of being overrun. Your men fought bravely."

The Captain acknowledges the complement. "We are happy to help the American government. Two of my men were wounded, but we killed six of the MS-13 dogs. We sent a squad to track them back into the jungle and we'll try to locate their headquarters. But we should increase your security detail."

Michelle smiles. "Thank you Captain. We would appreciate the help. We still have to get to the American embassy tomorrow, but then we'll probably be leaving your beautiful country to get back to the U.S. as quickly as we can."

The Major expresses surprise. "I thought the EMP blasts have devastated your country?"

"We have to get back there soon. But first things first. We have to get to the U.S. Embassy. Thank you again for your support Captain."

The Belizean Captain gives Michelle a brief bow and orders his men to take up defensive positions before he leaves to return to his military base.

Michelle and Mark walk back into the hanger and sit to figure out their next steps.

Michelle starts the conversation. "We need to get to the Embassy today, and then if we can fly into Andrews AFB, we could get home tomorrow."

Mark nods. "The issue is what is left there and if we could get to the White House or our offices. I hope we can get in touch with S-Cubed or the President again."

"Well, let's get some rest and then get an early start. If we can get back to the U.S., then I think we can do more good there, than here. Plus I think MS-13 was just testing our defenses, I wouldn't be surprised if they are planning a major attack. Capturing this jet would be huge for their organization. We need to get out of here as soon as we can."

With that Michelle climbs up into the jet to get a few hours of sleep while Mark grabs his M-16 and steps outside to take up his defensive position.

Chapter 15

Tehran, Iran
August 24th

General Aziz just got off the phone with his Air Force chief; he is smiling. Aziz turns to his second in command. "Our ICBMs detonated at 300 km above the United States and have crippled the Great Satan. Unfortunately the North Koreans failed. All but one of their ICBM were either shot down by the American THAAD systems or failed in the launch. "

Lieutenant General Farrakh Rajavi smiles. "Yes, our sources in Canada tell us that the American communications system is down nationwide. The electrical grid is dead. There are riots starting in many of the major cities."

"Have there been any reports connecting the ICBMs to us?"

Lt. General Rajai shakes his head. "No, since the missiles were launched from Syria, the CIA doesn't know for sure if it was the Russians, al-Qaeda or ISIL. We have started the disinformation campaign to point towards al-Qaeda."

"Ok, keep me informed of any changes and keep our military on full alert."

The Lt. General stands. "Yes sir!"

As he leaves, Major General Sassan Mokri enters and salutes. He is the head of the Revolutionary Guard Intelligence Department.

"General, I have some news about your daughter-in-law."

General Aziz looks surprised. "What do you have?"

"We have learned that your son's wife was either abducted or left voluntarily with a CIA operative. His name is Malis

Nasir Al-Din. He was taken to America as a child and became a CIA operative several years ago after being a Navy SEAL. His American name is Mark Aldin. Saarah is his sister. The ruse used was to wire her mouth shut and he took her out of the country as a Russian citizen. They flew to Germany for medical aid and at that point we have lost her trail."

The General nods. "She is of no consequence. My son has moved on. But I want you to find out how the CIA agent got into our country. If he can get into and out of Iran, he is a clear danger."

The Intelligence head nods.

"On another issue, Javad Tousi was killed earlier this week. Someone snuck into his compound, killed his two guards, and then slit his throat. Nothing was taken, so he was the target. As you know, he was the man who purchased your daughter-in-law and her mother. They lived with him for almost twenty-five years. The mother died just a couple of years ago."

Aziz nods. "Yes I know all this. I didn't agree with my son's choice for a wife, but it has worked out for him. He is free to get re-married and hopefully have children. Thank Allah he did not have children with that infidel. Could her leaving the country be tied to Tousi's death?"

"Possibly. We will continue to investigate, but so far there are few leads."

The General picks up a paper to read. "Ok, I want a report on what Israel is doing. We have six additional ICBM missiles with nuclear warheads that will be ready in four weeks. I want you to put together a plan to launch them at Israel in November. With America preoccupied with their EMP issues, this is the time to end the Israelis once and for all."

Chapter 16

S-Cubed Headquarters
August 24th

Ducky Duckworth's government jet is approaching Joint Base Andrews just outside Washington D.C. when the pilots hear the control tower's instructions; "Navy Alpha Golf three-two-one, maintain heading to runway 19L."

The pilot acknowledges, "Roger 19L."

The jet begins its gentle decent.

The control tower sends out a message. "Navy Alpha Golf three-two-one, we had an EMP event. Acknowledge."

The pilots are taken by surprise, but professionally reply. "Roger tower, we understand. What radar capabilities do you have? We will land on runway 19L as soon

110

as possible." They realize that they were fortunately just far enough off the coast when the EMPs hit, that the electromagnetic blast didn't affect their onboard systems.

"Navy Alpha Golf three-two-one, we have limited radar. You are cleared to land."

The pilots accelerate the jet to get to Joint Base Andrews as quickly as is safe. Runway 19L comes up fast as the pilots maneuver and drop the landing gear. As the jet hits the runway too fast, the pilots quickly apply the brakes and steer toward a military hanger.

As the plane was descending, Ducky could see multiple fires and lots of smoke throughout Washington D.C.

After the landing and taxi, the jet pulls into the hanger and Ducky unbuckles and moves to the jet door. The pilot opens their cockpit door and puts his hand on Ducky's shoulder.

"We just got notification of an EMP event."

Ducky shows his surprise, but understands the gravity of the event.

The pilots move back into the cockpit to shutdown the jet. Ducky runs down the stairs and heads for his 1984 Kawasaki KLR 650 that he left in the hanger on his prior flight out. He just hopes he can kick-start it.

He drops his go-bag and mounts the bike. He opens the choke lever and kicks the starter. The first two kicks produce nothing, but the third kick starts the engine. Ducky opens the throttle and the engine roars to life.

Grabbing his bag, Ducky pulls his Sig Saucer P320 and slaps in his 17 round magazine. He ratchets in a round and sets the safety. Then the Sig goes into the small of his back. Ducky pulls on his leather jacket and dons his helmet. Revving his

650, he pulls out of the terminal and heads for the main gate.

As he approaches the gate he sees a dozen Marines fully armed. Ducky knows most of them as he slows and nods his acknowledgement. The Sergeant moves forward. "Ducky, you really want to go out there? It's total chaos. Riots and looting. The army is just starting to move out to try to maintain peace."

"Yeah, but I have to get to work!" Ducky says with a grin.

The Marines open the gate and Ducky accelerates out onto the frontage road, then onto Suitland Road, then quickly to the Capital Inner Loop. Dodging stalled cars and trucks, Ducky makes excellent time, roaring over the Potomac River and into Alexandra. Suddenly he sees five large eighteen wheelers strung across the freeway and a large group of people standing in front of them.

Ducky slows to 30 MPH as he approaches. He knows most people would love to have his motorcycle, but he is determined to not give it up. He accelerates and pulls onto the grass medium bypassing the crowd and the truck roadblock. Back at over 60 MPH he avoids cars and the occasional pedestrian. After continuing up I-495, Ducky comes up on the city of Dunn Loring. It's a sleepy small town that he has driven through dozens of times. This time however, it will not be so easy. He slows as he sees several commercial trucks pulled across the highway. In front of the trucks is a group of at least twenty men and several women.

Several of the group starts towards him. Ducky looks left then right. He sees the Oak Street overpass, but it is behind the barriers. He makes a decision and guns the motorcycle cutting over the medium and up onto Railroad Street, he makes a hard right and accelerates to Oak Street then a left away from the freeway. Ducky turns onto Oak Street, then a right onto Gallows Road. Appropriate he thinks as he speeds past surprised residents.

Suddenly he sees a policeman standing in the middle of the street with his service revolver raised. Ducky slows and then stops ten feet from him. He flips his faceplate up and slowly pulls out his military ID.

"I'm military special forces, trying to get to my unit." Ducky lies.

The police officer lowers his gun. "What the hell happened? My patrol car stopped working as well as my radio."

"EMP, an Electro-Magnetic Pulse probably from Russia or China, I would guess. Only older models without electrical switches will start. Things will get out of hand really fast when the population figures out that there is no electricity, no communications and no real protection."

"Damn. I have to get back to my station. Can you give me a ride?"

Ducky sees that the cop is really young, probably in his early 20s and he knows that if the cop gets behind him he might realize he has a gun. Plus two people on the aging Kawasaki will slow it down. "Where is your station?"

The policeman has holstered his weapon and is trying to use his useless radio. "My station is in Arlington."

Ducky shakes his head. "I just came past there. Lots of roving gangs."

Just then Ducky sees five men approaching them. The policeman tenses and turns towards the group. As they get within twenty feet, Ducky can see that they are gang-bangers. All tattooed and walking with the swagger that indicated that they are packing.

"Stop right there!" Yells the cop. The leader steps forward. "We just want the motorcycle. Walk away and nobody gets hurt."

The cop puts his hand on the butt of his pistol. Ducky can sense that he is very nervous.

"Not going to happen!" Yells Ducky.

The men start to spread out slowly, step by step as they close in. Suddenly one of the men pulls out a gun and points it at the cop. "Pull out your gun with your thumb and forefinger and drop it on the ground. Real slow."

The cop looks to Ducky then reaches for his weapon slowly. "Give them the bike, not worth our lives."

Ducky keeps his eyes on the group and says under his breath; "they will take the bike, your gun and kill us both."

The cop looks back at the group now twenty feet from them.

117

"On three pull your gun and drop to the ground. Take the two on your left, I'll take the leader and the two on my right."

"Come on dude, give us the bike."

Under his breath Ducky says, "one, two three..."

At that point Ducky reaches behind him and in one smooth motion he pulls out his Sig and shoots the leader with a double tap into the chest. The cop pulls his revolver and drops and aims at the man to the leaders right just as he pulls his gun. Both shoot at the same time. Both suffer mortal wounds. The others start to reach for their guns in their waistbands. Ducky shoots the leader in the head, then the another the abdomen and another with a double tap to the chest. Finally just one is still standing. He puts his hands up. Ducky tells him to spread out on the ground, hands above his head. The man complies and Ducky moves over to the cop. He has a wound to neck, just above his protective vest. Ducky has seen many combat wounds and knows this young cop won't survive.

"Don't move." Ducky says as he approaches the prone man. He pats him down to make sure he doesn't have a gun, and then turns him over. What he sees surprises him. The man is a female, actually a girl looking to be about 17. She looks terrified. He pulls her to her feet.

"How did you get mixed up with this crew?"

The girls starts crying. "I am not in the gang, my brother is. He is over there." Indicating one of the men shot and quite dead. "He brought me along, we are just looking for food and water."

Ducky notes that there are people now coming out from the neighborhood. He has to make a quick decision. "What is your name?"

"I'm Kristen, Kristen Morales."

"Ok Kristen, get on the motorcycle and hold on. I can't leave you here. He puts his revolver into the front of his pants and kicks the motorcycle to life. As he climbs onto the Kawasaki, some of the men start to run towards them. As Ducky feels the girls wrap her arms around his waist, he guns the motorcycle and speeds away towards the S-Cubed headquarters just several miles away.

Chapter 17

White House Situation Room
August 25th

The President wants some answers. Unfortunately communications with the outside world is limited to specifically hardened military sites and several international allies.

"Mr. President, we have communicated to the Canadian government and also to England, Germany and Israel that the United States was attacked by both North Korea and probably Iran. The Mossad has told us that they have proof that the Revolutionary Guards' Quds Force disassembled three Russian ICBM missiles and transported them to Syria, then reassembled them. The Israelis are willing to release their proof to the international community."

The President is listening intently. He nods. "Ok, so we know that Iran is behind the EMPs, what are our options?"

General Seibert stands and moves to a large screen. "We have three viable options to us now. One is to set off three nuclear EMP devices over Iran and send them back to the 1950s. They do not have the resources like we do to recover quickly, however their people are not as dependant upon electronics but the immediate damage would be severe and would take Iran years to recover from. Our second option would be to rally the international community around sanctions that would cripple the Iranian economy. But this would potentially allow them to continue their nuclear ambitions. We believe that China and potentially Russia would support crippling sanctions." The General pauses and takes a sip of a bottle of water. "Our third option is a full nuclear strike on Iran. We have a military plan in place that would allow strategic strikes at the Iranian military and civilian nuclear development facilities. There would be significant casualties of both military and civilian personnel."

The President rises. "I don't give a damn! The Iranian EMPs have likely killed tens of thousands of Americans! Millions more may die due to their actions. This is an act of war! We have to strike back quickly and with overwhelming force!"

The President stalks around the Situation Room mulling over the three options with the eyes of the Joint Chiefs on the Commander-in-Chief.

"There is another option" Andy Cobb the Director of National Intelligence says while rising to his full six foot six height. "The sanctions would be too timid a reaction to what has happened. It would send the wrong message to our adversaries. A full on nuclear attack would be seen as an over reaction and would wipe out the Persian people and they don't want the Theocracy system any more than we do. The other option is a limited EMP attack of three nukes exploded over Iran which will disable their military and civilian infrastructure, but that again won't stop Iran from continuing to develop nuclear weapons and maybe using them again. But what I would like to propose is that we send in a team to surgically take down the Iranian government. There are moderate factions in the Iranian government that could take over if we can eliminate several key players."

The President leans back in his chair. There is complete silence around the table while every member considers this option.

"We can not execute assassinations of foreign government officials per

Executive Order 12333 which prohibits the act of state-sponsored killing of foreign officials." Says the interim Secretary of State James Chan who replaced Cindy Decker, when she resigned. Then he continues. "This Order, which was drafted in the mid-1970s has been maintained by every administration since President Ford. However Order 12333 is not practical because the Order does not pose substantive legal restrictions to military options and allows the President the flexibility to employ the most brutal of tactics should he deem necessary." Chan says with a smile. "Therefore, if the President declares war on the Republic of Iran, then all bets are off."

There are some murmurs of agreement, and then the President rises again. "I do not want to punish the people of Iran, but clearly the regime and the military leaders must be eliminated. Also, if

125

the surgical strike is not successful, we can always do the EMPs." Turning to DNI Cobb, the President says, "Andy, how soon could be put together a plan?"

Andy Cobb nods. "We can have a plan available to you within a few days."

The President smiles. "Ok, let's meet again when we have worked out the general plan. James, draft a statement that condemns the actions of North Korea, Iran and al-Qaeda. Let the Iranians believe that we will not act. In the meantime let's focus on the domestic issues."

Chapter 18

Belize

August 25th

Michelle rises at dawn having gotten five hours of sleep. She feels refreshed but would love a hot shower. After using the bathroom on the jet and brushing her teeth, she climbs down the stairs onto the hanger floor. The captain looks up from his cooking of eggs on a large skillet.

"Wow, that smells great!" Says Michelle.

"While I was out on my patrol, I had a couple of kids come by with a dozen eggs for sale. I bought them thinking we should eat something other than Belizean Johnny Cakes..." He says with a smile.

Suddenly Mark enters the hanger with a Belize General in tow. "We have a major problem.   General Cruz has intelligence that MS-13 is planning a major assault on this hanger with the intention to capture or kill us and take the jet."

The General nods.   "They have almost three hundred fighters massed just a few miles away, getting ready for their attack.   We can bring in the military to protect the hanger and you, but we can't keep the troops here indefinitely."

Michelle looks at Mark.   They know the amount of bloodshed that an MS-13 attack would reap.   "General, could you give us a minute to discuss this?"

"Of course."

Mark and Michelle move off to the side and conference.   "We are planning to fly to the States, why should we have a fire fight and have a bunch of people killed, and then fly out of here.   I think we should pack up now and leave."

Mark nods. "I agree. I want to get home and try to set things right."

Michelle turns to the General, "We don't want to put your troops at risk, so we will pack up and leave within an hour."

The General breaks into a big smile. "We would have protected you but you are right; many, many men would have died."

Michelle turns to the pilots just sitting down to eat their eggs. "After you finish, do an operational check and let's get out of here."

The pilots smile and wolf down the last of their eggs and Johnny Cakes, washed down with fresh orange and mango juice.

Michelle and Mark pack up all their gear as the pilot walks around the jet with one last check. The co-pilot is turning on the electrical system and doing a pre-flight check.

As Michelle puts the last of gear on the plane, Mark keys the hanger door and it rolls up exposing the jet. After hurrying up the stairs, Mark pulls and locks the door and then hops into his seat. He and Michelle watch as the jet taxies onto the runway, then the engines roar and the jet begins its roll out accelerating into the air leaving the beautiful country of Belize behind.

Michelle sits back and breathes a sigh of relief. "Next stop Andrews AFB."

Mark smiles. "The issue will be getting to S-Cubed. We should try to contact Jonathan or Ducky and see what the situation is there on the ground."

Michelle picks up the phone next to her chair connecting her to the pilots. "Can I call a phone number in the States from this phone?" After getting an affirmative, the S-Cubed number is dialed and Michelle waits to see if anyone is there and who will answer.

Chapter 19

Teheran Iran
August 25th

The Revolutionary Guard Corp (IRGC) has been tasked with preserving the Islamic Republic of Iran and the safety of the Iranian government and Mullahs. The Quds Force is the Basij militia within the IRGC. Basij literally means "mobilization" and it is their mission to export the ideology of the Islamic Revolution worldwide by working directly with Hezbollah, Hamas and al-Qaeda. But additionally, the Quds Force is tasked with protecting the regime against foreign invasion and to suppress domestic anti-regime activity through intimidation and violence as necessary.

General Hamid Aziz leads the IRGC and has just promoted his son Sajad to the position of Commander of the Quds Force. Many in the Iranian Quds are not happy with this decision, but to question the General's decision would put their career and possibly their life in jeopardy.

The room is deep within a secure bunker inside the Fath Airbase just south of Teheran. In the room are the Iranian military brain-trust who control life and death in Iran. Each man is in charge of a specific aspect of the Iranian military including the armed forces, the air force, navy, Quds Force and intelligence.

The country is on war footing. After launching the three ICBMs from Syria, General Aziz expected an immediate military response from the United States or their lapdogs Israel. But what has happened is nothing so far. This has surprised Aziz.

So he called for a meeting with all of his top military leaders. "As you all know, yesterday we launched three ICBM missiles against the imperial devils of the United States. These nuclear missiles detonated at two hundred miles over the U.S. delivering an Electro-Magnetic Pulse that has knocked out all of their modern electronics; including their electricity grid, their water system, their telecommunications systems and has crippled the government. We have successfully crushed America!"

At that, the military men all stand and cheer. General Aziz breaks into a broad smile.

After the cheers die down, the General indicates for the men to sit. "We still have to be diligent. America even through it has been wounded, it is still very dangerous. We are unsure yet, how badly the EMP has affected the country and its government. But so far, reports out of Canada indicate that the EMP did the job we were hoping for. There are riots already in many of their large cities. Transportation

133

has been stopped. No electricity, clean water will be an issue within a month."

"Our Russian brothers tell us that their analysts believe that internal society breakdown will occupy the government resources over the next year or so. They felt that there was a forty percent chance that internal groups of disaffected Americans will overthrow the current government and install a more socialistic model."

"Americans are soft. They are more interested in their feelings, their social media image, they do not work hard, they are too dependant on their cellular phones and laptops. Now that those devices no longer work, their society will breakdown into chaos. America will go up in flames!"

The group cheers again.

One man raises his hand. He is the commander of the Iranian army. He has been in power for the past thirty years and commands over 200,000 men.

"Yes, Major General Saman?"

"Commander Aziz, I understand that the United States has launched a military operation against North Korea for their launching ICBMs against the U.S., Japan and South Korea. Do you believe that they could do the same against us?"

General Aziz still standing, starts to stroll around the room. "North Korea is a weak country with a weak leader. Their people are starving, they have no real manufacturing, no natural resources, they failed in their mission and they are paying for it now. The American military will crush North Korea."

Major General Saman nods. "I am going to speak candidly. If the United States decides to invade Iran, we are not equipped to defend ourselves. What if they shoot nuclear weapons at our key cities? A wounded animal is most dangerous. Our people for the most part will not fight in the streets against the Americans. The Mullahs know this. The Supreme Leader knows this. I personally believe this operation has put our country in great peril."

Many of the members sit in surprise at the candor that has been expressed.

General Aziz is quiet for several moments, and then speaks. "Major General Saman, are you questioning the decisions by the Supreme Leader? Do you question the decisions made by the military leadership of which you are a member?"

The Major General knows he is on shaky ground, but now he must continue. He is unsure how many of the group will support him, but he has spoken with at least ten of them and they support his call for Aziz to step down. "Commander, many of us do not agree with your decisions. We would ask for a vote of confidence."

There is dead silence. General Aziz continues his slow walk around the large table. "So, who of you are not satisfied with my leadership?"

Nobody raises his hand or stands. General Aziz nods.

Suddenly Major General Saman stands at attention. "I will be the first to stand."

Nobody else moves. Aziz moves to behind the Major General and draws his pistol and places the muzzle against the back of the man's head.

Looking around, Aziz sneers. "Who else is willing to stand against me?"

In the quiet room, they hear Commander Aziz cock the PC-9 ZOAF 9mm semi-automatic pistol. As he waits, all of the men look into the eyes of the Major General who now knows he has no support.

The gun shot startles all of the men. Blood and brain matter splatter all over the

137

table while Major General Samans' lifeless body slumps onto the floor.

The General holsters his pistol and continues his walk around the room. "Are there any other issues you wish to bring to my attention?"

There is just silence as the men rise and walk quickly from the room.

After all of the men have left the room, General Aziz smiles at his son Sajad. "You were right. Ten traitors in our military upper command. But with Major General Saman out of the way, our plan to destroy Israel can now proceed. With the EMPs that we delivered; America will have a Jihadi white Christmas."

Chapter 20

S-Cubed Headquarters
August 24th

An alarm suddenly goes off throughout the building. The clanging is deafening. In the S-Cubed control room the guards are watching a motorcycle approaching at high speed on their monitors. The high resolution cameras set up on the perimeter picked up the intruder just as the motorcycle breached the security area.

"Two riders, approaching at 60 MPH!"

Two of the guards grab their MK-17 assault rifles and rush out of the front doors. The two receptionists, former Army Rangers also raise their MK-17s ready to back up their team members.

As the motorcycle approaches, both guards aim their rifles with a shoot to kill order.

Suddenly the motorcycle comes to a skidding stop and the driver throws off his helmet and raises his hands. The guards are surprised but recognized the driver as Ducky Duckworth.

"Just coming back to work. I didn't know I would get a reception like this!" He says with a big smile.

The guards lower their guns and walk slowly towards him. The passenger gets off the bike and they see she is a young girl. As Ducky walks his motorcycle into the lobby, he is met by Jonathan Bardsley.

"Quite the entrance..."

Ducky smiles, "Well, there are lots of angry people out there after the lights went out."

Jonathan slaps Ducky on the shoulder. "Glad you are back!"

"What is the situation here?"

The Communications Specialist pulls Ducky to the side. "Michelle and Mark were on their way back when the EMP hit. What's up with the girl?"

Ducky looks back at the girl sitting in the lobby being given a soda and some snacks. "On my way from Andrews I ran into a group of gang-bangers. A cop was there and the leader of the gang pulled a gun on us wanting to steal the motorcycle. I had my pistol and we defended ourselves, unfortunately the cop was killed but we killed all of the bangers except for her who didn't have a gun. I thought she was a guy, but was wrong. I couldn't leave her in the chaos, so here she is."

Jonathan nods. "Ok, we'll take good care of her. Our emergency generators worked great. Also our hardened site over our servers and computers was able to keep everything working. A few laptops and cellular phones were fried if they were too close to the windows, but otherwise we are still in communications with the NSA, CIA, FBI and most of the military sites. The billions the Federal Government spent on hardening those facilities are paying dividends now."

"Have you heard from Michelle and Mark since the EMP?"

"Yeah, they are in Belize."

Ducky smiles, "Must be nice! Laying on a beautiful beach, lots of sunshine and warm Caribbean water. We may never see them again!"

"They will be coming back as soon as they can. We should hear from them later today or tomorrow."

"If they come into Andrews they will need an armed escort to get them here in one piece. There are lots of roving gangs out there looking for food, water and weapons." Says Ducky.

Jonathan leads Ducky up to the third floor where they sit in the conference room and try to figure out how to contact Michelle. Suddenly the phone in the conference room rings. Jonathan gets up and answers the call. "S-Cubed."

"Jonathan, this is Michelle."

"Wow, Ducky just arrived and we were trying to figure out how to contact you!"

"Mark is with me. What is the situation there?"

"Our systems are working as well as can be expected. We have communications with most of the major military sites, the NSA, CIA, FBI and the Situation Room at the White House."

"Excellent."

"I heard that you and Mark are in Belize?"

"We were there, but MS-13 wanted to steal the jet, so we decided to bail. Didn't need to get into a fire fight."

Ducky pipes in. "Are you coming into Andrews?"

"Yeah, should be there in about six hours."

"I just flew in and it was rough getting through the city. The highways are barricaded with semis and lots of gangs roaming around. Most are armed. If you can, get a military escort to S-Cubed."

Michelle and Mark both say "Thanks" at the same time.

"Can you contact the President and see if he can pull some strings to get us transportation from Andrews?"

Jonathan speaks up, "Absolutely!"

"Is everyone there safe?"

"Yes, we are doing well. Kelly is tracking events in North Korea and trying to track the three missiles from Syria. He

believes the Iranians are behind the launch,
but wants proof. He is tracking back
through satellite photos to find out who
brought the missiles in."

Michelle responds, "Ok, keep him
digging. If anyone can put together the
puzzle, it's Kelly. Check with the President
and I'll call you once we are on the
ground."

"Ok, talk to you then."

"Bye guys, see you soon."

With that, Michelle hangs up the
phone and sits back in her seat. "What do
you think?"

Mark takes a sip of his diet Pepsi
and considers the situation. "I hope we can
get a military escort. I wouldn't want to
fight it out with U.S. citizens."

"I agree, I'd prefer to take out some
of the guys who caused this mess. Let's get
to S-Cubed and then kick some butt."

Mark smiles. "I love it when you get excited about killing bad guys! Very sexy!"

Michelle smiles demurely and bats her eyes.

Chapter 21

White House Situation Room
August 25th

The President is sitting in the Situation Room with his Joint Chiefs and senior staff. The condition of the United States of America is now becoming clearer. The HEMP attack has crippled the basic infrastructure of the country. Almost ninety percent of the electrical grid is down. Water supplies will become critical within the next two weeks. Food is running low especially in the major cities that have seen riots and arson as law and order has broken down.

"What is happening with the National Guard?" Asks the President.

"We have activated every unit and they are being deployed. They will work in conjunction with the local police to maintain order and distribute food." Replies the Chief of Staff Randy Smith.

"What about the military?"

"We have decided to hold our regular military personnel at their bases at this point. But they are ready when needed."

The President rises, "God damn it, we need to get things moving; food, water and medical supplies. What about the electrical grid?"

Randy Smith looks down at his notes. "We are having problems even finding let alone communicating with the heads of the electrical companies. Some were in their offices, others on their way to their offices and some on the West coast were home. But of course all of their communications devices went down with the HEMP. We have sent National Guardsmen to their offices and homes and hope to at least get

148

some of them to the White House to figure out what to do."

The President sits back. "What about tracking down who shot the ICBMs from Syria?"

Andy Cobb, the DNI leans forward and opens a file on the table. "We have proof that the Iranians received nine ICBMs from Russia in March. They were shipped from the Russian port of Makhachkala on an oil tanker on the Caspian Sea to the Iranian port city of Rasht. The ship was loaded at night and unloaded at night. They were trying to hide the six ICBMs. They were all disassembled in crates marked as auto parts, electrical equipment and medical supplies. We tracked the crates on a dozen different trucks to their TAB (Tactical Air Base) 2 near Tabriz. Of course we didn't know they were ICBMs, but now it is clear that they re-shipped the crates to Syria along with the nuclear warheads and re-assembled them on the launchers."

The President interrupts. "So they fired three ICBMs at us, what about the other six?"

Cobb nods. "I think they are held back the six in case the first three didn't reach their targets, or they plan to fire them at Israel in a preemptive strike."

The President stands and starts a slow walk around the Situation Room. "So what are our options to punish the Iranians?"

Cobb looks up from his notes. "We can't definitely prove that Iran launched those ICBMs. We destroyed the launchers and killed everyone there. We have a Special Ops team there now collecting evidence, but it will be months before we can prove it was the Iranians. But we have a plan to send in a small team to take out General Hamid Aziz and work with the leaders of the Iranian Green Seculars (IGS) to overthrow the current Iranian government. The IGS is committed to a more secular government and improved relations with the West. Our other option is a war with Iran. Millions will die and really, we are not in position to act militarily."

The President stops pacing. "Who is involved?"

Andy Cobb smiles. "Our main participants should be landing at Andrews right now. Michelle Samaha and Mark Aldin will lead the operation. They will take a hand picked team into Iran, link up with the opposition group, then assassinate Aziz and as many of the top military as possible and then get out of the country. They will put together the details of the plan and have it ready for your approval within a week."

"Excellent. Keep me updated. Let me know immediately when Michelle

Rik Thistle

Samaha checks in", the President says while standing, then leaving the room.

Chapter 22

Joint Base Andrews, Maryland
August 25th

Michelle and Mark walk down the jet stairs and are greeted by Colonel Max "Dragon" Waters. He is the commanding officer of the 11th Wing and Joint Base Andrews. He is a legend as a fighter pilot during several campaigns including Desert Storm and Enduring Freedom.

Michelle extends her hand and shakes Colonel Waters hand with a strong handshake. He smiles. "Welcome back to the United States of America."

Michelle smiles too. "Glad there is an America to come back to."

Colonel Waters shakes Marks hand and notes that he handles himself like a Navy SEAL.

153

"Well, they hit us hard with three EMPs and took out a lot of the civilian electronics and there are riots and emergencies all around the country, but the military and the National Guard are mobilizing and we'll have order restored within a few weeks."

Michelle, Mark and Colonel Waters walk from the jet and into the administration building with several enlisted men saluting as they pass.

"We are anxious to get to our building and start planning an operation authorized by the President."

"Yes, I was contacted by the President's chief of staff. We were told to give you whatever assistance you require."

Mark and Michelle smile. "Great, but we need to try to contact S-Cubed and let them know we arrived safely and will be there shortly."

"Of course. Fortunately the military had hardened most of our communications systems throughout the country in anticipation of an EMP attack. So we are able to maintain our command and control operations despite the pulse damage."

They arrive at the Colonel's office and he shows the duo to a conference room next door. "You should be able to get through to your guys from here." He closes the door and attends to another issue.

Michelle picks up the phone and dials Jonathan Bardsley's phone number. After two rings she hears a familiar voice. "Hello, Bardsley here."

"Hi Jonathan, its Michelle."

"Oh man, are you guys ok?"

Michelle smiles. "Yes, Mark and I landed just a few minutes ago at Andrews and we'll be coming over there shortly."

Jonathan responds. "Ducky got here yesterday and says it's really freaky out there. Lots of roving gangs. Plus Ducky came in on his motorcycle with a surprising package."

Michelle scrunches up her brow, "Glad he made it there safely, but a surprising package?"
Jonathan laughs, "Yeah, you'll see when you get here."

"Ok, we should be there in an hour or so. We'll get a military escort, so it shouldn't be too exciting. See you soon."

Michelle hangs up and turns to Mark. "Ducky made it safely. Now let's get to the office so we can map out a plan to hit the Iranians back."

"Roger that. I want to take a real shower too and get some chow."

They leave the conference room and find a Major waiting to help them with their transportation.

"We have a Cougar 6X6 MRAP vehicle that we are confident will get you safely to your offices."

Mark is very familiar with the Cougar vehicle. It has a crew of two and can carry up to ten fully armed fighters and has a top speed of 65 MPH. It is armored and has gun mounts on the top that will intimidate any foe.

"We'll have four armed Marines with you, plus one M240B medium machine gun on top. That should keep any bad guys at bay."

Michelle nods. "Sounds like we are in good hands."

They walk outside and see the Cougar sitting outside with four Marines standing nearby. They are introduced to Michelle and Mark and they all enter the Cougar MRAP interior. The drivers are in position as is the gunner on top. Mark and

Michelle take their seats as do the Marines in their full combat gear.

They feel the vehicle start to roll but it is tough to see through the small sized armored windows. But Michelle and Mark can see them leaving the base and driving along a highway. Michelle spots hundreds of abandoned cars and trucks. But she also sees large groups of people standing on or near the highway watching the military vehicle pass by.

Suddenly the vehicle is rocked by an explosion. The Cougar MRAP is designed to take on improvised explosive devices, but this one is a big one. The Marines are used to IEDs, but not on American soil. Michelle can see a dozen men running towards the vehicle with various guns. Their communications ear buds suddenly come alive. "Combatants approaching on each side. Lay down warning shots."

"Roger"

Suddenly Michelle and Mark can hear the loud explosion of the M240B machine gun spiting out rounds over the heads of the men.

The men hit the ground and the Cougar vehicle starts up again. A man stands and throws a grenade and it bounces off the vehicle then explodes. Many of the men then rise and rush the vehicle. The driver accelerates but then men on an overpass drop a flaming barrel of tar. The barrel hits the front of the vehicle and explodes with tar all over the windshield.

Michelle is expecting to hear the machine gun, but it is silent. One of the Marines climbs up and sees that the gunner had been badly burned by the flaming tar. "Gunner has been hit. Taking him down inside."

Mark moves immediately and helps the Marine pull the gunner down. He has severe burns. The squad medic begins immediately medical treatment. At the same time Mark climbs up the stairs into the machine gun turret. Swinging around the machine gun, he trains it on a man pulling another grenade from a bag. Mark pulls the trigger and the gun spits out multiple rounds that cut the man in half. He drops the grenade and it explodes taking out three others nearby. Mark then swings the gun to the other side and lays down a line of death on a dozen men running toward the vehicle. After the initial salvo, Mark swings the gun around again. He sees an older pickup truck coming at them fast. In the bed are half a dozen men with shotguns and AK-47s. Mark trains the M240B at the vehicle and lets loose. The rain of bullets hit the front of the truck disabling the engine while multiple bullets take out the driver. The truck explodes as the fuel line ignites then the truck rolls to a halt just twenty feet from the Cougar.

Mark swings around and sees a dozen men running away. "Ok to exit vehicle and get the tar off the windshield."

The remaining Marines exit guns raised in a protective circle. One of the drivers leaves the vehicle and tries to scrap the tar from the windows. He is fairly successful and after a couple of minutes he can see where they are going.

One of the Marines takes over for Mark and the vehicle rumbles forward and heads towards the S-Cubed headquarters.

"What about Mac, we should head back to the base," Mark says, referring to the gunner.

The medic responds, "The wounds aren't as bad as I originally thought, some second degree burns on his arms. He is going to be ok. We can drop you guys off and then head back."

After twenty minutes, the vehicle pulls to the front of the building and Mark and Michelle step out. They thank the Marines and then hurry into the lobby to be greeted by Jonathan Bardsley, Ducky Duckworth and Kelly Campos.

Chapter 23

Tehran, Iran
August 26th

At the Fath Air Base, Lieutenant General Farrokh Rajavi is standing in a large aircraft hanger. Inside he is monitoring the loading of three ICBM missiles sections that have been disassembled for transport to Syria. Each missile has been carefully packed in containers marked with a Green Crescent and the Arabic words for hospital supplies.

The Lieutenant General walks slowly past the convoy, inspecting each vehicle while the Quds force men stand at attention. Towards the end of the line is a specially designed vehicle that is lead lined. It contains the three nuclear weapons that will be installed on the missiles just prior to launch.

"When will you be ready to leave?" Rajavi asks the Major leading this operation.

"Everything is ready. We are just waiting for dusk so that we can drive to the Iraqi border. We'll cross at Al 'Amarah, then use the back roads to As Salman. We will then set up in the desert with tents covering our assembly of the missiles on the launchers. Then we'll await your order to launch."

The Lieutenant General smiles. "Right now we will launch two at Israel and one at Saudi Arabia. I want the nuke to hit directly over the Iman Turki Bin Abdullah Grand Mosque."

"Yes, sir. We have targeted the missiles to hit Tel Aviv and Jerusalem."

"Excellent. Good luck Major, may Allah guide you to a successful operation."

The major bows slightly, then straightens and salutes.

164

Rajavi walks back out of the hanger and to his armored car. Sitting inside, he calls General Aziz on a secure phone. "General, the missiles are ready to be transported; they should be in place within two weeks."

"Excellent. When you get back to headquarters, we need to discuss another issue."

The Lieutenant General frowns. "Yes sir, I should be back within an hour."

Chapter 24

Los Angeles, CA
August 26th

After four days of eating the food that was in the refrigerator and now some of the frozen food that is no longer frozen has kept them well fed and feeling ok about their situation.

Jennifer has broken up some of their wooden furniture to make a fire in the patio area of her house. They have enough water for another couple of weeks, but then what? She has spent several sleepless nights guarding the downstairs while Mary slept upstairs in her room. Jennifer wished she had a gun, but when Mark left she told him to take all his guns with him. She hated that he was so comfortable with those weapons. But she knew that her

166

husband being a Navy SEAL, it was his job. But even after he left the SEALs and started teaching at UCLA, he would go to the range to practice. He took Mary occasionally and she became a pretty good shot, much to Jennifer's horror.

"Why aren't the cars working?" Asks Mary.

"The EMP fries all electronics within its blast area. That could be all of the western United States as far as we know. So no transportation, no food delivery, no medical supplies. I wouldn't be surprised if there aren't riots in Los Angeles."

"Mom, we are really close to downtown." Jennifer can hear the fear in her daughter's voice.

Suddenly there is a knock on their front door. Jennifer moves to a side window and sees three men standing on her porch. One is looking in the front window.

Jennifer moves slowly from the window and motions to Mary to be quiet.

"Anyone home? We need some food and water. We have money to pay for it." One of the men yells through the door.

The door handle rattles as a man tries the door. Jennifer looks at the 2x4 piece of lumber she had found in the garage and wedged under the door handle and the staircase. They could break a window to get in, but they don't know if the homeowner has a gun.

Jennifer whispers to Mary "go upstairs and lock yourself in the bathroom, don't come out until I tell you to, do you understand?" Mary nods then starts up the stairs, then stops and whispers. "Maybe we should give them some water and then they will go away."

Jennifer shakes her head. She knows human behavior better than most. If these men know there are only two women

Jihadi White Christmas

in the house, they will be targets for the most primal of instincts.

They stand still for several minutes, and then Jennifer moves to the side window. She sees the porch empty and she breathes a sigh of relief.

Chapter 25

S-Cubed Headquarters
August 26th

Mark and Michelle enter the headquarters to hugs and whoops of relief. Michelle hugs Jonathan, Ducky and Kelly. Then Mark turns to the young girl standing shyly behind the three S-Cubed members.

"So who is this?" motioning towards the young girl.

Ducky smiles. "This is Kristen Morales. She was with a gang that tried to take my bike. She wasn't armed and she would have been in danger if I had left her on the street."

Michelle moves forward and extends her hand. "Hi Kristen, my name is Michelle. If you follow the rules, then you can stay here until the government gets things

170

under control. If you violate any of the rules, we'll send you back to your neighborhood. Understood?"

Kristen nods.

"Ok, we'll set you up in one of the offices. My assistant will arrange for clothes and food."

"Thank you. If there is anything I can do to help, let me know."

Michelle smiles. "Thanks honey, we'll see if there is anything you can do."

Michelle then turns to the team. "Let's get upstairs and start to pull together a plan that was requested by the President."

Michelle's assistant takes Kristen to an unused office on the second floor while the rest of the team heads to the top floor and the main conference room.

Jonathan had placed some snacks and water on the table. "I spoke with the President yesterday. He wants our team to

171

put together a plan to disrupt the Iranian government and bring General Aziz and the top military leadership to account for their actions. If the Iranian theocracy falls; then all the better."

Michelle nods. "Ok, we all agree that the Iranians launched three Russian ICBMs to affect an EMP event over the United States. They killed thousands of Americans with that event. Then they have probably led to tens of thousands more Americans dead at this point through the riots. Millions could die in the next weeks or months if the government can't get this situation under control."

Mark stands, "Ok what can we do from here?"

Kelly Campos interrupts. "I did some snooping around the Iranian military computers and was able to infiltrate their mainframes and placed a Trojan horse program that will allow me to peruse their

172

past files.   I have confirmed that the Supreme Leader and Aziz approved the use of the ICBMs and that they have been working with North Korea for the past decade."

Michelle smiles. "Can you get that information to the CIA and the President?"

'Will do." Kelly says as he leans his six foot six frame back in his chair.

"So how do we topple the Iranian government?" says Michelle.

Mark pulls out a folder and reads the report prepared by the Joint Chiefs. "Well, they sent over three options. One option is to lob three ICBMs of our own and create an EMP event over Iran. Send them back to the 1950s. That will allow the President to argue proportionality with the world powers. The second option is an all out attack. At this point, it might stretch the military to pull it off. We could destroy Iran and their military, but millions of civilians would die too. It would be a tough sell to the rest of the world. But it would send a strong message to any other adversary. The third option is to send in a small team to take out the Iranian military leadership and the theocracy. Cut the head off the government and make sure more moderate leaders rise to the top. The President will have to make the final decision."

Michelle stands as Mark sits. "Are there any other options?"

Kelly Campos lends forward. "With some work, I am sure I could take down their electrical grid. Maybe not permanently, but certainly it would take them months to get the juice flowing."

Michelle nods. "OK, start working on that and any other way you can think of to cripple their economy."

I'll speak with the President. In the meantime, put together an operation for option three. Are we all in agreement?"

Jihadi White Christmas

Everyone nods and then stands.
"Ok, let's get to work!"

Chapter 26

Anju, North Korea
August 26th

The North Korean generals watch the main screen as the missile tracks streak towards the United States. Kim Jong-Un is excited like a kid at Christmas; jumping up and down and clapping his hands with a big smile on his face.

The generals know the missile tracks are faked for the benefit of the Chairman and to keep them alive. Off to the side both Generals can see a separate monitor that is keeping track of the dozen missiles launched. Several misfired and either didn't get off the launch pad or exploded while in flight. Some did reach their designated altitude and started on their descent, but then the Air Force lost communications

176

with the missiles. It could only be assumed that the American missile defense system shot them down. But that could not be revealed to the dear leader. That would result in their execution.

Kim Jong-Un regains his composure and turns to the Generals. "What is happening with the South Korean and American forces on our soil?"

General Gim Chi-Sung stands at attention. "Chairman, we have ordered all 3.5 million of the Red Guards to repel the invaders. They will fight with knives, pitchforks and whatever they can to stop the invasion."

All of the Generals know it is a losing strategy. They are just playing for time. The people have been starving for the past forty years, plus no citizen of North Korea could own a gun. That was punishable by death, and many people had been executed when a neighbor or family member turned them in for some extra food. It was amazing what people will do when they are starving.

Kim Jong-Un nods. He looks tired and somewhat disoriented. "Chairman, why don't you have something to eat and lie down and rest, we will keep you informed of any new developments."

The Chairman smiles. "Yes, of course. Wake me if there are any significant changes."

The Chairman and his personal aide leave the room for a well appointed stateroom that has a king sized bed, a full shower and a large screen television with over one hundred movies available.

As soon as the leader leaves the room, the Generals move to a conference room adjacent to the control room and close the door, pulling the blinds.

The three Generals stand silent for several seconds, and then General Ri begins.

"All of our missiles were either shot down or misfired. If America wanted to totally destroy us, they could. I believe they will just invade and then we can sue for peace. They will want leaders they can trust to help rebuild the country."

General Jeong Jha-Ji nods. "We can capture Kim and offer him to the Americans if they will guarantee our and our families' safety."

General Gim looks shocked. "What are you talking about? I saw the missiles hit the United States soil. We just killed millions and millions of Americans. We have to fight to the death!"

General Ri and General Jeong smile. "General, you saw a video game. The missiles didn't hit anything. It was a big farce. If we showed the Chairman the failure of the missile system, we would all be dead right now."

General Gim sits down shaking his head. "What have you done? You have deceived the Chairman! When I tell him, both of you will be arrested!"

General Jeong moves behind the outraged General Gim, while at the same time pulling his Russian made GSH-18 Parabellum Pistol.

General Gim is shouting now, spittle spraying from his mouth. "This is an outrage! THIS IS TREASON!" Suddenly General Gim notices General Ri moving to the side and realizes that General Jeong is behind him. He starts to stand when the bullet enters his brain. Brain matter and the front portion of his skull explode across the room. His body slumps onto the conference room table with a sickening thud. The gunshot inside the conference room is loud and the officers in the operations room all turn and look but can't see into the room.

General Jeong holsters his gun and pulls the body off the conference room table and onto the floor.

"We need to get in communications with the Americans. Make our offer." Says Jeong.

"I will start that process. It might take us several days to convince the Americans that this is not a ruse."

"Ok, get it done. I will get several of my most trusted men and we will sedate Kim and restrain him. I'll take a digital photo of him that we can send to the Americans along with our proposal."

The two Generals walk out of the conference room and lock the door hoping that their gambit will not only save their lives, but their country.

Chapter 27

Washington D.C.
August 27th

The President is still in the Situation Room under the White House. He is meeting around the clock with his military directing the war against North Korea while at the same time waiting for the plan from S-Cubed to take their revenge on Iran.

"What is our status on the ground in North Korea?" Asks the President.

"We have totally overrun the DMZ and have a battalion on its way to Pyongyang, sir." Answers a major charged with monitoring the forward troops and mechanized division.

The President turns to his DNI, "What about Kim?"

The Director of National Intelligence shakes his head. "No communications within North Korea regarding Kim. Mostly trying to reposition troops to meet our surge."

A bird Colonel enters the Situation Room and approaches the President. "Mr. President, I have a communication from S-Cubed."

The President takes the piece of paper and reads the note. "Ok, I have a video meeting in ten minutes. Colonel, I'll take the video conference in my office."

"Yes sir. I'll set it up."

The President turns to the DNI and his CIA chief, "Let's meet in my office in ten minutes. I'd like you both to hear the S-Cubed plan."

With that President Baker leaves the Situation Room and walks down the corridor to his Presidential office under the White House.

After a few minutes the secure phone buzzes and the DNI picks up. "Yes?"

"This is Michelle Samaha at S-Cubed for the President."

"Yes, hi Michelle, this is Andy. I heard about your trip to Italy and locations south. Sounds like the operation was very successful."

"Hi Andy. Yes we were able to get everyone home but did have one fatality."

Andy Cobb nods. "Yes, very unfortunate but we are very happy the President's family is safe. Also I heard you eliminated the black widow."

Michelle smiles. "Yes sir. We are happy the whole operation went well. We have a plan for Iran that we are confident will be successful."

"Yes of course. I'll put you on the speaker phone for the President."

Jihadi White Christmas

With a push of a button, the two groups are connected over the speaker phone.

"Good morning Michelle. Thank you again to you and your team for getting my family home safely. I will always be in your debt."

"Thank you Mr. President. We have a solid plan to get into Iran and extract some revenge for their nuclear missile launch."

"Great, the nation is currently hurting directly because of the Mullah's actions. We need to make sure the Iranian leadership knows they can't fuck with us again! Sorry for the language Michelle. With me are Andy and Cam Anderson."

"That is ok sir, I've heard worse. Hi Cam, glad you are safe. So our initial plan is to use a small mini-sub called a Proteus to take us to the Iranian coast near Teheran. We will work with the CIA to determine the best insertion location. Then we will have our agent there pick us up and take us to a safe house in the city. We'll have our own arms, ammunition and communications equipment."

"What is Proteus?" Asks the President.

Michelle hits a button to bring up a photo on the large screen in the Situation Room, while Ducky continues the explanation. "The Proteus is an underwater self-driving vehicle that is 25 feet long and 5 feet wide. It can carry six people with full gear. We will all be in full SCUBA gear and can dive to over 200 feet and travel for up to 700 miles. But the best thing about Proteus is that it can deliver its cargo and then wait off shore for us to call it back to a GPS coordinate and pick us up within two weeks."

"Excellent. What about your targets?"

Jihadi White Christmas

"We have four primary targets; General Hamid Aziz, Lieutenant General Farrakh Rajavi, President Ali Khomeini and Mohsen Rezaee Mirgha'ed the head of the Islamic Revolutionary Corps. We know that if the leadership is taken out, there are factions within Iran that will revolt and take over the government. Those groups are more willing to normalize relations between Iran and the United State. Taking out all four at the same time will be extremely difficult. But we have a plan to create a situation that will put all four in the same room. If we can do that, then our operation can be successful. Otherwise, we'll take out as many as possible and then hope that Proteus will find us before the Iranian Revolutionary Guards do."

At the pause, Mark speaks up. "Mr. President, this is Mark Aldin. What is the current situation around the country?"

"Hi Mark, glad to hear you are safe. Thank you for your efforts to save my daughter and grandkids. They are safe here." The President continues. "The EMPs knocked the country to its knees, but we are responding. We believe we can get the electrical grid back online for most of the country within the next several months. We have the military delivering food and water to the hardest hit cities. The National Guard and our military are trying to maintain order in the urban areas. Unfortunately millions will probably die over the next month, but by October I believe the crisis will be manageable."

Mark responds. "Thank you Mr. President. We are ready to take the fight to the Iranian leadership."

"Ok, good luck Michelle, Ducky and Mark. We will pray for your success."

Chapter 28

Los Angeles, CA
August 27th

It had been a long sleepless night for Jennifer. She slept downstairs while Mary slept in her room. It was now almost 6 am and she is very hungry.

Jennifer stretches her arms above her head then leans down to touch the floor with her palms. She wishes she could brew a cup of strong coffee to help her come fully awake.

Suddenly she hears the kitchen door knob being giggled. Jennifer stands and tenses then grabs the Louisville Slugger of her ex-husband leaning against the stairs. Trying to be as silent as possible, Jennifer slips into the living room and peers into the kitchen. From her vantage point, Jennifer

189

can't see the door, but she can see a shadow of someone at the door.

Standing quietly, she suddenly catches movement to her right and sees a man moving in their backyard. This image sends a chill down her spine. It is the same man who tried yesterday to get into the house.

Jennifer starts to move silently back towards the stairs when suddenly the back door explodes inward. Within seconds two men rush inside. Jennifer grabs her bat and backs against the hallway door.

A large man with a torn t-shirt and a five day beard looms in the hallway. "Well, well. I guess you are here alone little lady. We watched the house all night and didn't see hubby come home. I guess he is either not in the picture or was killed during the nuclear attack."

Jennifer is now backing away, and then suddenly backs into another person.

Jihadi White Christmas

She screams as her arms are grabbed and she drops the bat.

The main leader almost lifts her off the floor. He is incredibly strong. Jennifer can smell his sour breath on her neck. "I asked you for some water and some food, but you refused. Now we will take what we want. Do you understand lady?"

Jennifer nods her head while trying to get herself back under control. "Take what you want and go."

The man laughs. "Yes, we will take what we want, but we might not leave. This is a very nice house. You must have a rich husband. Probably old and fat? Does he take care of all your needs?" There is a pause. "I didn't think so."

Jennifer is now shaking, knowing her life and the life of her daughter is in jeopardy. "Please, just take our food and water and move on."

A third man moves into the hallway. He is younger and watches as the older man moves his hands over Jennifer's body.

The man slips his hand inside Jennifer's blouse and she feels his hand roughly massage her breast. He squeezes her nipple and says, "Our food and water? Is there someone else in the house?"

Jennifer mentally chastises herself for the slip of her tongue. She can feel his erection pressing against her.

The leader looks around the den and sees multiple photos on the wall. Several photos feature Mary, including one in a prom dress. "Ah, you have a daughter. Is she home?"

"Check upstairs. She might have some kids up there." The leader says.

As the large man starts up the stairs, suddenly Mary appears at the top of the landing holding a 9mm Glock. It is pointed directly at the man's chest.

Jihadi White Christmas

"Hold on there little lady." Says the man holding up his hands. He continues to slowly move up one step at a time. "I only wanted to check on you kids to make sure you are ok."

The revolver doesn't waver. "Let go of my mom and leave our house." Mary says in a low steady voice.

"Come on kid. Put the gun down and we can fry up some eggs and bacon for breakfast. After that, we'll leave."

The man takes another step and is only three steps from the landing.

"One more step and I'll shoot."

The man half turns towards his partner. "Geez, I guess the little lady is serious."

Suddenly the man turns lightning quick and leaps towards the landing and Mary. There is a shot, then another. The hallway and stairway is suddenly filled with gun smoke. The man had reached the

193

landing and is blocking Jennifer's view of her daughter. Jennifer screams, and then watches as the man topples backwards down the stairs. At the same time, Jennifer brings her leg up and backwards and lands a perfect kick to the leader's testicles. He immediately pulls his hand from her blouse and bends over, but still maintains a hold of Jennifer's arm. Mary steps down the stairs with the gun on the second man. "Get out of our house!" screams Mary.

The man catches his breath and then smiles. "You bitch, you killed my brother." Pulling Jennifer towards him, "now I am going to rape your mother while you watch and then rape you little darling."

The two shots startle Jennifer, but then she feels his hand loosen his grip. The man stands for a second then collapses with one shot through his forehead, the second through his throat. He is dead before he hits the floor.

Jihadi White Christmas

The third man runs from the hallway and is out the back door before Mary can re-aim her Glock.

Mary starts to cry and sits on the stairs cradling the gun. Jennifer steps over the body on the stairs and pulls her daughter to her. "It's ok baby, it's ok."

They sit together crying for several minutes, and then Jennifer wipes her nose with her sleeve. "Come on, we have to take these bodies outside and bury them. Then we have to fortify the doors and windows, so that nobody else can get in until order is restored."

With that, both women drag the bodies out into the backyard and find a shovel and start to dig a big hole.

Chapter 29

S-Cubed Headquarters
August 29th

Mark and Ducky have been toiling over the Iran plan for the past two days to make sure every contingency has been covered. Mark called the commander of the Naval Special Warfare Center located at Panama City, Florida to request the use of two Proteus units. The commander was a former Navy SEAL and knew Mark from previous operations. The request was approved and the two units are being readied for shipment to Crete, where the operation will be launched.

"We will have to have a small team. Anything larger than six will draw attention."

Michelle enters the conference room and stands still looking at the white board and the dozen paper notes taped to the wall detailing each key element of their operation. "Ok, give me a summary."

Mark takes the lead. "The team will consist of six; you, me, Ducky, and three special operators that I have worked with before. They are all volunteers and current Navy SEALs."

Michelle nods. "What about the targets?"

Right on time, Kelly Campos enters the conference room taking up a big space just to the right of Mark. Even though Mark is a large man, he is dwarfed by the 6'6" 350 lb computer genius. "Hi guys! Anyone want a donut hole?" Kelly is wearing a tie-dyed shirt, shorts and sandals but fits in well with super-black operators.

Everyone declines and Kelly gobbles the last three donut holes, then continues.

"After the EMPs were detonated over the United States, the four main targets all went into hiding. They anticipated an immediate American response. Now a week or so later, each has surfaced. I was able to hack into Hamid Aziz mobile phone and have followed him over the past two days. As long as he keeps that phone, we should know his location at any time. The Lieutenant General Rajavi is in the same building at most times, I was also able to hack his phone. The issue will be with the President of Iran and the Supreme leader. I do not believe the Supreme leader uses a mobile phone. The President has an aide that carries a mobile phone and I've hacked that, but he isn't always in the same room as the President."

Michelle interrupts. "So we have to try to find a way to get all four in the same room."

Jihadi White Christmas

Mark puts down his dry marker. "That will be tough. Getting Aziz and Rajavi together would be tough enough, but all four is almost impossible. The only way to facilitate that would be to create a situation within the leadership that would bring them all together."

The four S-Cubed team members sit at the conference table and mull over multiple scenarios, suddenly Mark jumps up and starts to write on the white board. After several minutes he turns and smiles. "The one thing that would create a panic among the leadership is that if the Iranian people started a new Arab Spring. We have several agents in Iran and they can help to contact those moderate groups. Once the movement starts, those moderates in Iran who want a more democratic government will react. I am sure we can get millions into the streets calling for the Mullahs to step aside."

"We can enter the country a day or two before and be in position to take down one or more of the targets. In addition, maybe the revolt will take hold and could take down the government." Adds Michelle.

Kelly steps forward. "I know I am new here and I don't have any counter-terrorism experience but I think a social media campaign at the same time could get most of the younger people behind the revolt. Iran's population is 81 million and with over 50 percent being younger than 35. Those are the people that use social media and will be the leading force of any revolution."

Michelle looks at Mark and they both smile at the same time.

"What kind of social media campaign could you put together?" Asks Michelle.

Kelly now getting more excited about his role in this operation leans forward. "I can put together both Facebook and Twitter accounts that will criticize the Mullahs and the military for their bombing America. Put the facts out and let the revolution start organically."

"The issue will be the military and the Revolutionary Guard. They will want to keep power and will brutally try to put down any revolt." Says Ducky.

"That is why we need to take Aziz and Rajavi down simultaneously. If we can seed a revolt in Iran then all the better. But taking out the top Mullahs too would be best case scenario." Mused Mark.

"At the same time I can take control of their electrical system. I've already hacked in and turned out the lights in some cities, just for a few minutes so that the local officials don't suspect a Trojan Horse inside their system." Kelly says with a big smile.

"Excellent. Ok, let's put together the final plan and I'll brief the President. Let's plan to leave for the Middle East within the next couple of days. We'll have to arrange for a flight and get a vehicle to take us to Andrews AFB. The situation is still very volatile in the cities, but the military is distributing food and water and the number of riots has lessened. If the electricity can be turned back on, then I believe the nation will get back on its feet." Michelle says while she stands. "Also get in touch with the Mossad agent in Iran and make sure he is read into the plan. He will be key in making the whole plan work."

Chapter 30

Greenbrier Hotel West Virginia
August 29th

The President Pro Tempore and the Speaker of the House are on opposite sides of the political spectrum, but they are united in one common goal, the retention of power. When the current President won the past election, their collective power decreased and they were not happy.   Now this independent President has gotten them into a shooting war with the North Koreans. Who cares if Chairman Kim has nuclear weapons, the art of politics is to delay, delay, delay and commit to as little as possible.   But neither side can work with this maverick. He isn't beholden to anyone. There are very few pressure points that can be applied to make him do what either man wants. It's a situation that has to change.

George Watkins has been the Speaker of the House off and on for the past thirty-five years. As a Republican he is committed to conservative values but he is more committed to assembling power which he has carefully done over the past couple of decades. He is sitting at the elite Greenbrier Country Club in West Virginia. He and most of his staff and many of the Representatives and Senators were brought out to a government secure facility under the Greenbrier facility. After the EMP attack on the United States, the government quickly moved to secure the top politicians to this facility so that the government of the United States of America could continue to function.

George is sitting in one of the private libraries at the Country Club smoking his favorite cigar and sipping on a

204

glass of his favorite bourbon, Maker's 46. How did Baker get elected when both parties were working behind the scenes to stop him? Ultimately it didn't matter if a Democrat or Republican was elected; the powerful in the Federal government would continue to be in power. It's been that way since the Republic was formed.

"I imagine you are trying to think how we got ourselves into this mess." Says the President Pro Tempore.

Speaker Watkins looks up and smiles. "Hi Jordan. Have a seat and get a drink." He motions to the steward waiting discretely outside of ear shot. The black man moves quickly to the chairs and asks the Senator what he would like.

"Hi James, perhaps a glass of Blanton's Single Barrel bourbon with some ice."

As the steward moves away, Jordan Claiborne sits heavily and shakes his head.

205

The Senator from Illinois just can't believe the position they are currently in. "That asshole Baker has certainly made a mess of things."

Speaker Watkins nods. "Damn shame. We had the government humming without his interference. Our power was at its height."

The steward returns with the Senator's drink. "Thank you James." Taking the glass and then taking a long, slow sip.

As the steward leaves, Jordan Claiborne leans forward. "With the EMP, the President is about to declare Marshall Law. That will give him absolute power. We can't let that happen."

The Representative from Texas sits quietly for several moments. "Jordan, I agree. We are all stuck in this gilded cage while the real decisions are being made in the Situation Room under the White House."

The Senator takes a sip of his bourbon and settles back into his comfortable armchair. "The military is solidly behind the President, the population is totally cut off from any communications and the President is running the country by himself. He attacks North Korea, he allows nuclear weapons to be used against America and I heard about a hybrid virus attack. What else could go wrong? We have to stop him." Senator Claiborne leans forward. "What I would suggest is implementing the Black Flag protocol."

Representative Watkins looks up from his drink. "That protocol has only been approved by the committee three times."

Senator Claiborne looks around to make sure nobody is close enough to hear what he is about to say. "In the day,

Lincoln had to go. Then Kennedy was a clear and present danger to the Republic, he had to be removed. Then of course there was Regan. He was taking the country in the wrong direction. Unfortunately we weren't successful with that one."

Both men have been in Congress over the past thirty years and know that Presidents come and go, but that the real power brokers are in the House and the Senate.

"This is a critical situation, getting the committee together will take a few days, maybe a week. I'll get the military to bring each of them here so we can meet and present the facts and get their approval."

Both men take a long swallow of their drinks. With the decision made, both men rise to go to lunch together knowing with the country in crisis, it is up to them to right the ship.

Chapter 31

As Salman, Iraq
August 29th

Major Dabiri had led the caravan of six trucks over three days to As Salman, traveling only at night for eight hours at a time. With the caravan was a squad of Revolutionary Guards to protect this most precious cargo.

It's now almost 2 am when the operation radio crackled to life. "Major, we are reaching our destination in five minutes."

"Very good Sergeant. When we arrive, set up a half mile perimeter with personnel and sensors."

"Yes sir."

The major knows these missiles are a gift from Allah. These weapons will smite the enemies of the Republic of Iran. Within a week, the Republic will be ready to launch three nuclear missiles to destroy Israel and Saudi Arabia, plus have three more in reserve if they are needed.

Major Dabiri places a call to his commander even through it is in the middle of the night. "Commander Aziz, we have arrived at our destination and will begin assembly of the missiles as soon as possible. We should be ready in five days."

Hamid Aziz is not happy. "Fool, do not call me on an unsecured phone. When you have more information, use the secure phone!" With that, the Commander hangs up the call.

Even though it's 2 am, Aziz is still in his command office. Able to catch cat naps, the General is legendary for keeping odd hours. General Aziz turns to his second in command. "That Major should know better! Send a replacement immediately."

Jihadi White Christmas

The Major General salutes and turns
and leaves the room to carry out the
Commander's order. He knows it will result
in Major Dabiri being imprisoned or killed.
But he also knows that not carrying out the
order would result in his death.

This operation is too important to
mess up. He knows that American
intelligence is constantly monitoring all calls,
emails and texts. Should the Americans
discover the Iranian operation, they will act
immediately.

He places a call to a Colonel telling
him to get onto a helicopter and fly to As
Salman to replace Major Dabiri.

At the same time, 6,325 miles away
Kelly Campos has captured the telephone
conversation and the location of General
Aziz by tapping into the NSA databases and
using Artificial Intelligence to comb through
the trillions of messages captured by the

NSA each minute for specific elements. One of those elements is the name Aziz.

Kelly picks up his phone and calls Michelle's office. "Boss, we captured Aziz's phone number and have a new call placed to Aziz. I'll send the audio clip up to you shortly. But it seems the Iranians are building more missiles and will be ready in five days."

Chapter 32

S-Cubed Headquarters
September 1st

Mark and Ducky have been tweaking the plan over the past several days; discussing key personnel, equipment, tactics, timing and extraction.

Michelle enters the office and both men smile knowing they are getting closer to an approval of their plan. "Good morning guys, what have we got?"

Mark walks over to a large white board with the operational plan key points. "Ok, the short story is that we fly from Greece to the Caspian Sea, drop into the water and have a previously placed Proteus mini-sub there to take us to the Iranian coast where we'll drive to Tehran for a meeting with the Mullahs and Aziz."

At this point Michelle says, "Whoa, how do we get to the Caspian Sea? How does the Proteus get us to the beach? Which beach? How do we get out of the water undetected and to a car to take us to Tehran?"

Mark smiles and looks to Ducky. "Maybe you should take the lead on getting us to Iran"

Ducky stands just as Jonathan Bardsley and Campos arrive and sit in on the meeting at the invitation of Michelle. "The team of six will fly to the Navy base on the Greece Island of Crete. The Naval Support Activity base on Souda Bay is about as close as we can get to Iran without causing any alarm bells in Iran. We will fly on a Navy transport over Turkey and Azerbaijan to the Caspian Sea. We have worked out a flight plan that has been cleared by both countries for a fly-over for humanitarian purposes to Turkmenistan to

deliver medical equipment and supplies."
Ducky puts up a large Middle East map
showing the flight plan. "While over the
Caspian Sea the plane will report a
mechanical issue and will drop to a minimal
altitude and the six passengers will
parachute out to a specific location
approximately sixty miles from the Iranian
coast. The plane will continue to its
humanitarian mission and then return to
Greece."

At this point, Mark stands and takes
the Dry Erase Marker. "Once we are in the
water, the previously deposited Proteus
mini-sub will rendezvous with us and we'll
enter the sub. At ten knots per hour, the
sub will take us to the Iranian coast within a
couple of hours. We will land on a beach
near the Ramsar Parsian Hotel beach."

"At a hotel beach?" Michelle asks.

"The hotel is up in the foothills. We
will arrive at 1 am on a beach that is near a

local road. It will allow us to change out of our scuba suits and into more local clothes and put the scuba gear in suitcases. Then we will check into the hotel for some rest." Says Mark with a big smile.

"Really? Check in?"

"Yeah, the local police will be suspicious of anyone traveling around at that hour. It's a small town of only 33,000 people and they will know most of the key people there. But a late arriving wealthy Swiss couple in a limo with their security team will be accepted. We have reservations for three of their largest rooms for the week. Michelle and I both speak French fluently and our cover is impeccable."

With that, Mark tosses the marker onto the conference table. "The next day, we'll have the limousine pick us up to take us to a meeting in Tehran."

Michelle looks surprised. "A limousine?"

"Well, as a wealthy businessman, his wife and four guards it would be the only way he would travel." Mark says with a wide smile.

"So the pickup in Iran will be by our Limousine?"

"Yes, at 2 am, we'll be picked up near the beach and taken to the hotel by a Mossad agent in a rented limo. Then the next morning we'll travel to Teheran to a meeting with Aziz and the top Iranian leadership."

"Just like that?"

Mark smiles, "Yep, just like that."

Chapter 33

Washington D.C. White House September 1st

The President and many of his top aides have moved back up into the White House from the Situation Room and the PEOC, the Presidential Emergency Operations Center, now that the immediate threat of a nuclear war has passed. Secure communications within the military which was hardened decades ago is operational.

The military has taken control of most of the major cities. Rioting has died down. Food and water and basic supplies have started to flow using military vehicles. It is a monstrous job that only the military with its precision could accomplish.

The electrical grid is being fixed by thousands of electrical company workers toiling in twelve hour shifts. It's slow work. With over 120,000 miles of transmission lines and thousands of transmission stations, it's a daunting task. Moving from electrical station to station, the workers are replacing those components fried in the EMP attack. Fortunately many of the electrical companies had taken heed of warnings by the CIA and security officials about the danger of EMPs, and over the past twenty years had secretly hardened many of the key faculties within the electrical grid.

Randy Smith, the President's Chief of Staff is meeting with the five major North American Regional Councils that control ninety percent of the power grid. Each has come to the White House to report on their progress.

"So let me get this straight, after almost two weeks you only have twenty percent of the grid operational?"

Jack Hayes, the Chairman of the NERC responds. "Yes sir. But we are accelerating our progress. Just getting the proper personnel into place was a major issue. But now we are confident we can get power to most of the major cities within the month and throughout the United States by the end of October."

The Chief of Staff nods. "Is it a matter of money?"

"No, we each only have limited experts in this area. But the Western Interconnection of Western U.S. is at almost forty percent, the Eastern Interconnection is at thirty percent, and the Texas Interconnection is at over fifty percent. However the MRO and RFC covering most of the Midwestern states are less than ten percent each. Riots in some of the major cities such as Chicago, Detroit, Cleveland, Milwaukee and Baltimore slowed down our progress. Roving gangs threatened electrical trucks and we had to withdraw our efforts until the military gained control."

"Ok, do you need military escorts?"

"Sure that might help getting our crews to the key facilities and keeping them safe while they're working."   Says the Chairman.

"Ok, I'll make some calls and we'll get protective details for your crews. Send me a list of who, when and where."

"Yes sir. We'll get those lists to you later today."

Randy Smith stands suddenly, "Ok, thanks for coming in." With that he turns and leaves the Roosevelt Room and walks down the hall to the Oval Office. Upon entering, he sees the President with his feet up on the Presidential desk reading a report.

"Mr. President, I just met with the NERC leaders and they are confident they can get the electrical grid operational throughout the U.S. by the end of October."

221

The President shakes his head. "Damn, but I guess at least the heat will be on before winter hits."

The Chief of Staff slumps into the chair opposite the President. "Yeah, things are improving. We are using the military to move food, water, medical supplies and other key materials. The transportation companies are fixing their trucks, communications companies are starting to broadcast to those that have electricity and slowly the country is getting back to somewhat normal."

The President sits back in his chair and takes his feet off the desk. "We need to hit back at Iran. I know we have a black operation in the planning stages, but I want to do something now!"

Randy Smith nods. "But Mr. President, until we can produce definitive proof that Iran launched the Russian missiles we can't publically retaliate. Privately that is another story."

At that point, the President's secretary knocks and enters the Oval Office. "Mr. President, Michelle Samaha has arrived."

Chapter 34

Washington D.C. White House
September 1st

The President stands and greets Michelle Samaha. "Hi Michelle, good to see you."

"Thank you Mr. President. We have a solid plan to get into Iran and try to cause some mayhem."

The President moves to the couch and signals Michelle to sit opposite him. Randy Smith continues to stand watching the interaction.

"Do you want details or just a summary?"

The President smiles. "A summary will be fine."

Michelle refers to her notes, then starts. "A team of six will enter Iran. We will arrange for a meeting with the

Supreme Leader and Aziz and as many top Mullahs we can get there. At the same time we'll create a social media storm for the population to overthrow the government. We'll have moderate groups ready to take over if there is a coup after we take out as many of the bad guys as we can."

The President is silent for several seconds. "Sounds pretty ambitious."

The Chief of Staff stands there in disbelief. "This sounds like a fantasy. If you are caught you'll all be executed. How do you arrange for a meeting with the Mullahs and with Aziz? How do you get out of Iran?"

Michelle looks at the President. "Mark Aldin will pose as a Swiss banker. I will be his wife. We'll have four security guards with us of course. The reason for the meeting is to discuss their accounts in Switzerland and their scheme to double their holdings by buying gold futures two

225

years ago, then creating a world crisis which has driven gold prices sky high. All of the top Mullahs and Aziz and his top aides have deposited Billions in the private Swiss bank; Habib Banque Zurich. They want an accounting and we'll give that." Michelle pauses then continues.

"After we have taken care of the top leadership, then we'll simply get into our limo and ride to the airport for a private jet ride back to Switzerland. If things go bad, then we'll use a mini-sub to leave Iran and get picked up in the Caspian Sea."

The President is pensive.

"Of course there are dozens of key details we'll have to put together, but we believe it is doable. We are depending upon the leaderships' greed to get us into the meeting."

The President stands. "Ok, get it done. I want to send a message to the world and if we can topple the Iranian theocracy, all the better.   Just don't get caught."

Michelle smiles. "We won't."

Chapter 35

Los Angles, CA
September 3rd

Jennifer and Mary are sitting in their kitchen eating hotdogs they had just cooked in their backyard fire pit.   Quite a lot of their furniture has been broken up and used for firewood.   It has kept them fed, but Jennifer hated to destroy her beautiful chairs and tables.

"How did you get the gun?"   Asks Jennifer broaching the subject they both have been avoiding.

Mary finishes her second hotdog and replies.   "Dad gave it to me when he left. He told me to keep it oiled and loaded in the event I had to use it.   I didn't tell you because I knew you'd make me get rid of it."

Jennifer nods, knowing that is true.

"Dad just wanted us to be safe knowing he would not be around to protect us. Sorry mom." Mary says with a sad look.

"Well, in this case your dad knew what was best for us. I am sorry you had to shoot those men, but if you hadn't I believe we'd both be dead right now."

Mary starts to sob, suddenly letting out the emotion she had kept in over the past several days. Jennifer takes her daughter into her arms and they both cry together.

"Mom, Dad gave me two guns. I have the 9mm, but he also gave me a Sig Saucer P226 that he carried in the Middle East. I can teach you how to shoot it if you want."

Jennifer looks at her daughter. She sure has grown up in the past month. "Sure honey, I'd like to learn so that we can protect each other."

Mary runs upstairs and gets the Sig and its ammo. She lays the gun on the kitchen table and begins to instruct her mother about how the gun works, how to load the bullets and then how to train the pistol on a target.

"Once you release the safety, you have to be prepared to pull the trigger. Aim for the chest since it's the largest area and is the easiest to hit. Don't hesitate."

Jennifer picks up the unloaded gun feeling how heavy it is. This was the first time she had handled a weapon. She was previously totally against any kind of weapon, believing that intelligent conversation would defuse any situation. It was just one of the reasons she and Mark split up. He was all about guns and getting the bad guys. Jennifer wished she could contact Mark, but she had no idea where in the world he might be. But clearly survival over the next couple of months is the most

Jihadi White Christmas

important thing for her and her daughter.
But now after what just happened in their
home, she knows that the world as she
knows it has changed. She nods to
daughter.

"Ok, tell me what I need to know."
Little did Jennifer know that within twenty-
four hours, her knowledge will keep both of
them alive.

Chapter 36

Anju, North Korea
September 4th

General Ri enters the Chairman's private room. The lights are low but he can see a form on the bed. He flips on the overhead lights and smiles as he sees Chairman Kim tied to the bed. Over the past few days, the Chairman had been drugged and kept captive.

The General moves to the side of the bed and looks down on the *Dear Leader*. Because of his families' treachery the people of North Korea have suffered greatly over the past sixty years. Kim il-Sung, grandfather of Kim Jung Un, declared the formation of the Democratic Peoples' Republic of Korea on September 8th, 1948 after the end of WWII. Over the past sixty years the Kim family starved its people to enrich themselves and keep the Kim family in power. The Kim family instituted the Songbun system. This divided the North Korean society into different social classes according to one's perceived loyalty to socialism and the regime. This classification determined the course of people's lives. The Songbun dictates the schools someone can attend, the occupations they are placed into and where they can live. Free speech became an offense punishable by imprisonment or even death. The worst part of this scheme was that if someone was arrested, up to three generations of their family would be sent to political prison camps.

Now the American and South Korean militaries are invading and easily taking town after town. The unification of Korea is now at hand. General Ri knows the people of North Korea already starving and weak, are no match for the two armies.

Yesterday General Ri and General Jeong did a video message that was sent to a CIA official that General Jeong had met while he was in Japan. He is unsure if this person was still working for the CIA, but he hoped he would get the message to the right people.

"He is our passage to freedom." Says General Jeong.

General Ri turns slowly and smiles. "I hope so. The Americans want him alive. That gives us leverage."

"Has the doctor been in this morning to monitor his vitals?"

"Yes, Doctor Lee visits him in the morning and in the afternoon to make sure the Chairman is comfortable and not in distress. He is of course being drugged in a twilight sleep. He can probably hear us, but not really understanding his situation.

234

Hopefully, within a couple of days we will have an agreement with the Americans and we can start to serve our country again."

General Ri steps away from the bed and nods. "Well, if the Americans won't agree to our proposal, then we'll have to kill Kim and head for the border. I know the Chinese do not want the Chairman there alive. He will create more issues for the Chinese then it will be worth."

General Jeong moves to the locked door. "We are running out of time. The Americans may be here within the next two days. I'll contact my CIA contact again. If I don't hear from him within the next six hours, I'll try to communicate directly with the White House."

Both men exit the room and lock the door. A loyal guard is posted by the door and snaps off a sharp salute as the two Generals walk down the hall towards the main communications room.

Chapter 37

Washington D.C. White House
September 5th

The President has just met with many of the top electric company executives on the progress getting the American electrical grid back up online. He is encouraged. Over the past week, electrical workers have spread out throughout the United States to replace and repair those interconnections for each regional hub for the North American Electric Reliability Corporation. Power is slowly starting to come on in city after city. With electrical power; unrest has decreased, riots have been stopped, food and water is now beginning to be delivered in the major cities by the military.

As the last of the executives exits the Oval office, Randy Smith the

President's chief of staff enters. "Mr. President, we just received a very strange phone call. It was from a person saying he is General Jeong Jha-Ji. He says he is calling on behalf of the people of North Korea.

The President frowns. "Could it really be Jeong?"

"We have a Korean expert within the Department of Defense questioning him. He will call me if he believes it really is General Jeong."

"How is it going in Korea today?"

"Mr. President, I know you have been focused on the electrical system, the American cities and the riots, but our military successes are stunning. We have overrun most of the regular North Korean army. We are within ten miles of Pyongyang and should have the city under our control within the next several days. The people have been starving. We are bringing food and medicines with our advanced forces. This has helped to pacify the population.

Suddenly Randy's phone rings. "Yes, ok I'll let the President know."

The President sits forward, "Is it really Jeong on the line?"

"Yes sir. The analyst has had some limited contact with him about twenty years ago and the General was able to answer questions only he would know."

"Ok, let's see what he wants."

With that, the President's phone rings and the President answers. "This is President Baker." Then the President pushes the button to activate the speaker.

In slow, careful English General Jeong begins the most important telephone call of his life. "Mr. President, thank you for taking my call. I will get right to the point. General Ri Pyong-Chol and I have captured Chairman Kim and are willing to turn him over to the American government for several concessions."

The President looks surprised. "How did you capture Chairman Kim?"

"We are in a secret facility outside of Pyongyang. When Chairman Kim laid down to rest, we drugged him. I can send you some photos showing him restrained."

"Ok, what are your concessions?"

There is a short pause, then the General speaks. "General Ri and I would like your word that we and our families will be given immunity from war crimes. Also we would be allowed to maintain any monies we have in foreign banks. If those conditions are acceptable, we can bring the war to an immediate halt and would be willing to work with the American and South Korean militaries to integrate into one Korea."

The President raises one eyebrow.

"That maybe acceptable, but I want to discuss this with our Generals. Can I call you back later today?"

There is another pause. "I will call your office in six hours. Thank you Mr. President."

With that, the phone line goes dead.

"What do you think?"

"I think they know they are about to lose the war and want to negotiate the best terms they can with their most important collateral."

"Ok, call the joint-chiefs and get them to the White House. I'd like to discuss this in an hour and be ready to end this war. It will save lives and allow us to dictate terms to China on a unified Korea.

Chapter 38

Crete Naval Base – Souda Bay
September 6th

Michelle, Mark, Ducky and the three SEALs are settling down in the naval base at Souda Bay in Crete, Greece.

Carrying all their gear in waterproof black duffle bags that are stuffed with their formal wear, weapons and other required items, the six move into an empty barrack for some food and rest to get ready for their insertion into Iran.

Michelle and Mark meet with the base commander and they map out the plane ride, drop, and submarine ride to the Iranian coast.

"The plane is being fueled and will be ready in an hour. With the current flight path you will be over the insertion point at approximately 22:00 local time." The Commander points with his finger.

"The two Proteus subs have been dropped by a separate plane several hours ago and will be ready for you when you hit the water."

Michelle and Mark look over the map and nod. "Looks like a good plan. What about extraction?"

"Well, you'll have to communicate your availability to the Proteus. It can come to shore with just ten feet of water. Here is a watch for each of your team members that shows your GPS position and in turn the position of the Proteus. Just get into ten feet of water and the Proteus will find you wherever your are."

Michelle smiles. "Excellent. Hopefully we'll all be together, but if we have to split up, this will allow each of us individually to be picked up."

Mark takes one more look at the map then stuffs it into his jacket. "Ok, let's brief the team and get ready to move out."

The two exit the Commander's office and walk across the base to the barrack. Upon entering the room each of the team members gets off their cots and gather around a large table.

Mark pulls out the map and he slowly goes over the plan step by step. At the end of stage one, he pauses. "Any questions?"

All of the SEALs have hundreds of operations under their belts and know a well planned op when they see it. They all shake their heads. "Looks good to me." Says the SEAL leader.

Michelle looks around the room at these warriors. "If you have any concerns, let's hear them now. This will not be easy. "

After a few seconds of silence, Mark turns and grabs his ruffle bag. "Ok, let's go!"

All of the men grab their bags and follow Mark and Michelle onto the tarmac and enter the C-130 Hercules. It has been previously stocked with medical supplies with just enough room for Michelle and her team and their HELO gear. Traveling over 2,400 km, it will be a long flight and a long drop to the Caspian Sea. Mark, Ducky and the rest of the team lay back on their duffle bags and try to get some rest. It will be almost four hours to the drop.

The C-130 powers up and lifts off the runway, but Ducky is already asleep.

Chapter 39

Washington D.C. White House
September 5th

The President has assembled the Joint-Chiefs, the CIA director and the DNI. They are all standing in the Oval office, examining the photos sent by General Jeong.

"Amazing. He looks totally secure."

"Are we sure these are not photo shopped?" asks the President.

The CIA Director responds. "Yes, we are sure they are actual digital photos taken with an iPhone camera. The photo was taken just five hours ago. It has a digital time stamp."

"Ok, so we can take control of Kim and his generals will help us to end the war.

What about their money in off shore accounts?"

"We believe that Ri and Jeong have approximately $500 million each in various Swiss banks. This is miniscule compared to what the Kim family has. So I think that getting their cooperation would not only save lives but would speed up the unification." Says the DNI Andy Cobb.

"What do you think General?" The President directs the question to General Seibert.

The General nods. "With their help we could wrap up the war within a week. Thousands of lives on both sides would be saved. Also, they can give us intelligence on any of their biological or chemical weapons. The money aside, ending this thing quickly would be worth the effort. I would vote to do the deal."

The President sits quietly for several seconds, then stands. "Ok, communicate with Jeong that they have a deal. Find out their location and we'll send a company of Rangers to make sure their troops will stand down and then take control of Kim and get him to the U.S."

After that, the real hard work will begin to try to reshape North Korea.

Chapter 40

Tehran, Iran
September 6th

General Aziz has finally come home. His wife has prepared a meal and the General has invited his son and his new potential daughter-in-law for a relaxing dinner.

Sajad Aziz is on the rise. With the help of his father, he is now in charge of the famed Quds Force. Sajad was concerned that his former wife's abduction would reflect badly on him, as he knows his father was not happy with his choice but was delighted when Sajad quickly chose another woman to wed.

After a dinner of family talk, the General and his son move to a well appointed study filled with classical books.

Jihadi White Christmas

Hamid moves to a closed hutch. Unlocking one of the doors; he swings it open and reveals hundreds of bottle of wine, scotch and whiskey that he had sent to him from overseas. Being a Muslim, he can not openly drink alcohol since it is prohibited by the Qur'an. But in private, the General has hosted parties where almost everyone had a drink or two.

"Sajad, do you want a drink?" Hamid says while pouring a generous portion of whiskey for himself.

"Yes, thank you father. I'll have the same."

The General pours the drink neat and hands it to his son. They sit in overstuffed chairs opposite each other. Hamid takes a sip and sits back. "We must prepare for the Americans to attack us. They will figure out our ruse eventually, but hopefully not before we destroy Israel and Saudi Arabia."

Sajad nods. "America has been brought to their knees. It will take them a year or more to recover. By then we will have nuked Israel and invaded Saudi Arabia."

"A proposal from my staff says that we must follow the Russian model. When Russia invaded Crimea, they said that the native peoples of Crimea were Russian, that they wanted to be Russian. There are 15% of the Saudi population that are Shia and will support our invasion. We have spies inside the Kingdom and they tell us that if we hit the House of Saud hard and kill all of the top leadership, then the general population will rise up and demand a theocracy similar to Iran. We will float the potential of a Caliphate by combining the two countries under Muslim law." Says Hamid.

Sajad takes a sip of his drink and feels it burning down his throat. "I am preparing the Quds Force to lead our attack. We will slip multiple Special Forces into Saudi Arabia to attack the Saudi leadership while at the same time assassinate the Supreme Leader and the President."

General Aziz smiles, "This plan has been in the planning stages with only six people within Iran knowing the details. Hamid had hoped that the Red Death virus would have destroyed the non-Persian population around the world, then eliminate the Iranian leadership and make it look like it was a desperate attack by the West. The people of Iran would need a leader and the General would be in position to control Iran. But their hybrid virus was stopped and the world knows it was an Iranian scientist that developed the Red Death. Now, with nothing to lose, Iran is prepared to take out Israel and take over the Saudi oil and control of the Muslim holy sites. It is a bold move.

"We must move quickly. The Americans will not be distracted for long. I want to strike Israel and the House of Saud within the next two weeks."

The General's son finishes his drink and sets his glass down. "I will make sure our people are ready. At the same time, we have to time our elimination of Supreme Leader and the President to implicate the Israelis."

"How will you do that?"

Sajad smiles, "We will arrange for a secret meeting with the Supreme Leader and the President. At the meeting we will include those on the Council that we don't trust. I will have our Quds Force in charge of security. We will have to sacrifice some of our men, but we will make it look like an Israeli bomb destroyed the room and killed the Iranian leadership."

"Excellent. At that point I will take charge and lead the Iranian people."

Chapter 41

Los Angeles, CA
September 7th

Jennifer and Mary are starting to run low on food and water. They have no idea what is going on in the country, Southern California or Los Angeles and their imaginations are taking flight. While eating a peanut butter and honey sandwich on stale bread, Mary takes a sip of a bottle of Costco water. "What happens when we run out of food?"

Jennifer has been thinking about this for the past several days. "I can try going to the Westin's house tomorrow morning, or maybe the Kellogg's house."

Both neighbors are on either side of the Aldin house and both are older people. "I should check on them anyway."

Rik Thistle

Their neighborhood is affluent with many business owners or professionals. Most are older without children at home. Jennifer has stockpiled all of their food into their walk-in pantry. They have several dozen cans of soup, some bags of chips, two cans of tuna and other assorted food stuffs that might keep them fed for another week or so. They have plenty of water at this point with two cases of water and a dozen cans of diet Pepsi.

After thinking about it, Jennifer says, "I think I should go check on the Westins and the Kelloggs now."

The sun has just started to set. There is still plenty of light but within an hour it will be dark and another night of potential terror.

Mary is sitting at the kitchen table, next to her is her 9 mm revolver. "I should go with you."

Jennifer considers the offer. "You might be right. Let's go now while there is still enough light."

Both women rise and move to the back door. "Let's go out the side gate and try the Westins first."

Jennifer and Mary enter the backyard and walk along a shaded path past their swimming pool and reach the side gate. Jennifer turns to Mary and whispers. "Let's take it slow. If we see anyone on the street, we come back and try tomorrow."

Mary nods while Jennifer opens the gate. It is a seven foot wooden door with a latch. Opening the gate, Jennifer and Mary exit the backyard and walk slowly past large pine trees and many bushes that Jennifer now knows could hide a person easily.

Mary has her Glock in a defensive position, her safety off but her finger not on the trigger.

Both women enter their front yard and Jennifer glances left then right. She doesn't see anyone on the street. "Let's go." Says Jennifer.

They move quickly on the sidewalk to the front walkway to the Westin house. The home is of course dark with no light coming from any of the front windows. Jennifer comes up to the front door and knocks. While they wait, Mary scans the street. After a fretful minute, Jennifer looks into the front window. The living room is dark and she doesn't see any movement.

Jennifer knocks again, then says quietly "June and Frank, its Jennifer Aldin and Mary. Are you guys ok?" She waits for another minute with no response.

"The Westins might be out of town, let's go around to their back yard and check that out."

The women move around the house and enter their next door neighbor's back yard. They also have a pool and spa and a well appointed barbeque. Suddenly Jennifer sees their back door open.

Jennifer stops, then points to the back door. Mary nods. Silently, the two move slowly towards the door. Jennifer peeks in and doesn't see anything amiss. As she steps into the kitchen she smells the stench of death. Mary can smell it too as she tightens her hand on the revolver.

The two creep inside. Inside the kitchen, Jennifer can see the pantry door wide open. She looks inside and sees that it's been cleaned out. After checking out the downstairs, Jennifer and Mary start up the stairs. It's starting to get darker and now Jennifer is beginning to get nervous. They top the stairs and move slowly towards the master bedroom. The door is closed. Jennifer listens at the door, and then knocks. "June, Frank are you there?"

She only hears silence. Jennifer tries the door and it opens. As she opens the door the smell is overwhelming. On the bed are the two neighbors both shot multiple times. Their blood has soaked the bed. Jennifer recoils and runs into Mary.

"Let's get out of here."

They retreat from the bedroom and quickly move down the steps. Mary now is more on guard scanning each room with her gun ready for one of the shadows to leap out at them.

They exit the house and into the cool air. They both take deep breaths trying to get their bearings. Mary had only seen dead people on TV. Jennifer retraces her steps out of the back yard and quickly moves to her home.

It is now fully dark and without street lights the darkness is complete. There is no real moon light so Jennifer takes her time, opening her gate and then closing it after Mary follows her in. They move past the pool and to their back door. It is open. Mary immediately steps in front of her mother. "Did you close it when you came out?" Whispers Jennifer.

Mary shakes her head then says, "I don't know."

The two of them enter the kitchen and look around. Mary closes and locks the kitchen door putting a 2x4 as a wedge to try to keep it closed. On the kitchen table is their flashlight. Jennifer grabs it and flicks it on. The beam cuts through the darkness. The pantry door is closed. They move slowly from room to room finally to the master bedroom. Looking in each closet and into the master bathroom and find it empty.

"Damn, we have to be more careful."

Their neighbors were killed for their food; it easily could have been them.

Although Jennifer hates guns she knows that their survival could hinge on her being able to use one.

"Get the other gun and teach me how to use it."

Chapter 42

Over the Caspian Sea
September 9th

At the appointed time, the C-130 radios on an open channel that they are experiencing a sudden depressurization and descending to 15,000 feet.

Mark, Jennifer, Ducky and the other three SEALs ready themselves for their High Altitude Low Opening jump. Jennifer has done some parachuting, but not a HALO. She is pretty nervous.

Over their communications link, each of the team members acknowledges their readiness.

The Lockheed C-130J Super Hercules aircraft slows to its minimum 115 MPH speed. The back door slides open creating a cold draft. Each jumper is attached to a jump line and shuffles forward to the jump point. Mark is in the lead with Michelle right behind him, then Ducky and the three SEALs all in line.

Mark keys his mic. "Michelle, your parachute will open automatically at altitude. Try to relax and enjoy the ride."

"Right. I'll be on your six."

At that point the group shuffles to the opening and jumps.   The cold air hits Michelle immediately.   At minus 12 degrees it would take your breath away, but Jennifer and the team have oxygen masks covering their faces. Michelle checks her altitude on her altimeter watch as she decends.   At 4,000 feet her parachute opens and she starts a slow descent.   She can see Mark ahead of her with his parachute moving in a slow zigzag motion.

They are maintaining radio silence until they hit the water.   After a few minutes Michelle notices the lights of the town coming up. Because the water is dark and there is no moon tonight, Michelle knows the water will come up fast.

Suddenly she sees a splash ahead of her and knows that is Mark hitting the water. She braces herself and slows her descent to just a couple of MPH. Then she sees the waves and hits the water. Jennifer slips under the water then pops up as her life preserver inflates.

"Alpha down." Mark says into his mic.

"Beta down" says Michelle.

Then each member of the team acknowledges that they are in the water.

Mark keys his Proteus GPS signal and waits. He believes they are within a quarter mile of both Proteus subs. Only one will approach with the second sub in reserve in the event of an accident.

Each team member swims to within a few feet of Mark. As they wait Mark keys the acknowledgement to the C-130 that they are down and in the water. He hears a two clicks acknowledgement.

Suddenly a large object surfaces next to Mark. He smiles as they open the hatch. Michelle scrambles in first, then Ducky, then the three SEALs. Mark is last and pulls the hatch shut. One of the SEALs is trained in the Proteus operation and takes control. He programs in the destination, and then sets the autopilot.

After two hours of undersea travel, the sub slows and the SEAL pilot lets everyone know they are just off shore. Mark keys his mic. "Let's get to the shore. I'll pick a dark spot where we can take off our wetsuits and stow them in our bags."

With that, they each disembark then seal the Proteus. As the team starts their swim, the sub drops under the waves and disappears.

They swim slowly with Mark in the lead. After ten minutes they can feel the tide pull and hear the waves gently crashing on the shore. Mark stops in five feel of water, raising his fist for the team to stop. He pulls his infrared binoculars from his bag and scans the shoreline. Even if a guard is not moving, Mark would still be able to see his heat signature.

Suddenly he sees a flash of light just down the beach. Mark stands silently watching the outline of the guard smoking a cigarette. After a couple of minutes the cigarette is extinguished as the guard continues up the beach. Mark waits a couple of minutes looking for another guard, but it is just black.

Mark motions them forward and the team wades the last twenty yards to the cobble stone beach. Each member hurries into the bushes just up from the shoreline. They strip off their wetsuits and reveal their clothes underneath. One of the SEALs moves up to the road and flashes his small light three times.

A large car starts up and moves quickly to beside the road. Each member scrambles to the limo trunk and throws their bags in. The Mossad agent welcomes Mark back to Iran, then slips behind the wheel and drives the team to the hotel.

As they arrive, a bellman still sleepy from being awoken with the surprise guests, take each of their bags and puts them on a cart. He notes that the bags are wet, but doesn't really think too much about it.

Mark in a suit and Michelle in a conservative pantsuit walk confidently into the hotel lobby. Mark smiles at the receptionist. "Bonjour, mon nom est Peter Monterie et c'est ma femme Michelle. Or I can speak in English if you wish. Sorry for the late arrival, we were delayed."

Jihadi White Christmas

The receptionist smiles. "English would be fine. Welcome to the Ramsar Parsian Hotel, your rooms are ready."

The *body guards* stand in a semi-circle around Mark and Michelle creating the impression of a wealthy man and his wife being guarded by hired guns. The room keys are given to Mark who then hands them off to the SEALs. They move quickly to the elevator with the Bellman and take it up four flights to the top floor. Mark and Michelle take the suite while the SEALs and Ducky split up to take the rooms on each side.

As they retire to their rooms, the first part of their plan has worked perfectly.

Chapter 43

The Greenbrier Hotel
September 9th

The old men sitting in a private study have been part of one of the most secret organizations that dates back two hundred years. In 1818 a small group of people in the United States government formed a CABAL to direct the Federal United States government when required.   The mythology of the word CABAL was from a group of government ministers in England that formed the cabal ministry in 1668 to make sure the government was steered in a particular direction. Those people were a part the ministry for King Charles II. They were Sir Thomas Clifford, Lord Arlington, the Duke of Buckingham, Lord Ashley and

Jihadi White Christmas

Lord Lauderdale whose initial letters spelled CABAL.

Since 1818 powerful American men were concerned about how the Federal government was being run. The treaty of 1818 between the United States and the United Kingdom established the northern boundary of the U.S. as the 49th parallel between Canada and the twenty United States. This Agreement created discord within the government. This small group felt that the United States could get more of Canada in the negotiation with England, but President James Monroe wanted peace with England and too quickly agreed to the 49th parallel the CABAL members thought. As the country spiraled into a civil war just forty years later, the CABAL felt they had to act. In 1858 the ongoing conflict between the North and South over the issue of slavery led the Southern leadership to threaten secession if the anti-slavery party won the Presidency. When Abraham Lincoln won the Presidency in 1860, the CABAL felt they had to act. It took them five years but eventually the President was assassinated by a stage actor, but it was the CABAL that was pulling the strings on his performance.

As members died or were deemed too frail to continue, the CABAL voted in new members to continue their goals.

Now the small group has met again, just the first time since 2001. There are just seven members. Like the justices of the Supreme Court, their appointment is for life. Each is a powerful man in his own right. Two are currently in the Federal government; Senator Jordan Claiborne and Speaker George Watkins, the third in line to the Presidency. The other members are from big business, the labor unions, the intelligence agencies, the national media and the Justice Department.

Jihadi White Christmas

Each has been summoned to the Greenbrier for this secret meeting. As each CABAL member arrives, they are given a white and black poker chip and their favorite drink.

George Watkins stands and walks over to the library door and turns the lock. Prior to the meeting, the Speaker had the room swept for listening devices just to be sure nobody can listen to their discussion. Each member had to give up their cellular phones.

"Gentlemen, I apologize for the short notice and you having to come here. But based on the events over the past two weeks, we have a very serious issue to decide."

All of the members look around the table and several take a sip of their drink.

"As you are all aware, the United States was hit with three Electro-Magnetic Pulse missiles that have crippled our country. Those missiles came from Syria but the intelligence agencies believe Iran was behind the launch. At the same time, President Baker invaded North Korea." The Speaker continues his slow walk around the large table.

"After Kim Jong-Un launched ten or twelve ICBMs at us." Says the Director of National Intelligence.

Senator Claiborne nods. "Yes, but the President was planning to invade anyway. Kim just gave him an excuse. The bigger issue is whether the President is fit to continue running the country." The Senator says in his Texas drawl.

The head of the largest union clears his throat. "Are you proposing impeachment?"

"No, I can not guarantee an impeachment vote by the Senate. Plus it might be months before the Congress convenes again. By then who knows what

272

mischief the President could get us into."
The Senator also stands. "I believe that
this President could get us into a shooting
war with China or Iran or both. He is a
dangerous man. He was elected by a fluke
and is not in my opinion the legitimate
leader of the greatest country in the world!"

Everyone in the room is stunned.
"Are you suggesting a Black Flag
operation?" Says the Supreme Court
Justice. He has been on the court for the
past thirty years and this is only his second
CABAL meeting.

Representative Watkins takes his
seat. "Yes, Senator Claiborne and I both
agree that because of the danger the
President poses, we must act. If we delay,
the Republic will be in jeopardy."

Watkins takes a sip of his drink, then
continues. "He is preparing to institute
Martial Law which will give him
unprecedented powers."

"How do you know that?" asks the CEO of one of the largest oil companies in the world.

"We have a very high source that has told us that Baker has spoken about it with his staff."

"Who is the source?"

The Senator smiles. "The President's Chief of Staff, Randy Smith has kept us apprised of everything going on within the White House. He told me yesterday that the President is about to order Martial Law. He will direct the U.S. military to take over all major key industries; electricity, water, transportation, financial, monetary and communications."

There is stunned surprise among the group.

"We are asking for your vote to authorize the Black Flag. The Congressman and I will arrange for the event, none of you will be implicated."

Jihadi White Christmas

The other CABAL members start talking among themselves. After a few minutes, the Senator asks for a vote. "If you agree with the plan, you will hold a black poker chip in your hand. If you disagree, you will hold a white poker chip. Each of us will hold out our hands in a closed fist. When I ask, all of us in order will reveal our vote. The majority rules so we'll need four black chips.

Each member pulls the two chips into their lap and considers the most important vote of their lives. As they palm the color of their choice, the CABAL leader asks them to hold out their fist. Each man raises his hand over the table, holding his chip.

Representative Watkins looks around the table. "Ok, reveal your votes in turn."

Speaker Watkins and Senator Claiborne show black chips. The Union chief shows his black chip. The oil executive shows a white chip. The Director of National Intelligence shows a white chip. All eyes look to the justice. He reveals a white chip. 3 -3 in votes. The last vote comes down to the national media executive. He grins and shows his chip. It is a black chip as he slams it down on the table.

"The President is a clear danger to the fabric of our country. We can not let him take absolute power. We must eliminate Baker" he hisses.

Senator Claiborne nods. "It is a tough decision, but you have voted and now we must act. Of course there can be no communications outside this room. Any breach will result in the ultimate penalty for you and your family. Am I clear?"

All of the CABAL members know that a few members over the years that revealed any information about the organization were quickly dealt with. They all voice their

affirmation.　　None　of　them　want　to
experience the wrath of the CABAL.

Chapter 44

Tehran, Iran
September 9th

A private message has come in for the President of Iran. The source is his private banker in Switzerland. Over the past twenty-five years, he and most of the Iranian leadership have discretely put away Billions of dollars and Euros taken from the Iranian people. Those funds are an insurance policy in the event there is a coup by the masses.

The President places a call on his secure phone to the Supreme Leader and to General Aziz. They received a similar message and are both waiting for this call.

"Should we take the meeting?" asks the Supreme Leader.

Jihadi White Christmas

"Yes, as you see the banker is concerned that America might recover more quickly then we thought and that would drop gold prices worldwide. Our gains based on our EMPs would be lost. I think we should see him and hear what he has to say." Says General Aziz.

The President of Iran can imagine the Supreme Leader thinking of why he should not be included.

"We should bring together all of the Mullahs too. Then everyone will have a stake in our decision." Says the President.

"I agree." Says Hamid Aziz.

The Supreme Leader finally answers. "The message says the banker and his wife and guards are already in Iran. They are staying at the Ramsar Parsian Hotel. Send some of the Quds most trusted men to bring them here."

"Yes Supreme Leader. I will arrange for the meeting for tomorrow."

Immediately General Aziz clicks off the call and places a call to his son. "We have just been given an opportunity to initiate our plan. There is a Swiss banker here to give us an accounting of our investments. I want you to send four Quds to escort them to the meeting tomorrow at the Presidential palace."

"Yes father. Should we install the bomb in room?" Says Sajad Aziz.

"No, send in a group of our four most trusted to guard the room. Then have him sweep the room as a show for the leadership. Then when I leave the room have the guards kill everyone there, including the Swiss banker."

"I will attend to those details father. I am confident we will be successful."

"The guards must kill everyone in the room. Nobody there can survive. Prior to the Swiss bankers' presentation, I will receive an urgent phone call and excuse myself from the room.   At that point the guards will shoot everyone and we will be one step closer to controlling the fate of Iran."

Chapter 45

Washington, D.C.
September 10th

The President strides quickly into the Cabinet room and moves to the head of the large conference room table.

"Please be seated."

After the EMP attack, life at least in Washington D.C. is starting to get back to a new normal. Over the past several weeks, the military has been successful in transporting millions of pounds of food to strategic distribution centers, where the National Guard has worked tirelessly to get food, water and medical supplies to residents in the largest cities. Riots have been slowed, with just a few hot spots where anarchists are still determined to bring the country down. But the

282

President's *shoot to kill* order for anyone looting has stopped all but the most determined or desperate.

"Ok, what have we got this morning?" Asks the President.

The Assistant Director of Homeland Security stands. "Mr. President. We have secured all of the top ten Midwest and Northeast cities, but Chicago. Although most of the city has been destroyed by fires caused by the rioting, they continue to refuse to allow U.S. troops within the city limits."

"What the Hell. Don't they know we are there to help them?"

The Chief of Staff, Randy Smith pipes up. "If you declared Martial Law then you would force their hand."

The President sits back to consider the advice. "Well, let's see how this plays out over the next couple of days and then I'll consider Martial Law."

"In the west we have a similar situation in San Francisco, Portland Oregon and Seattle. We are trying to work with the State and local governments, but of course with the lack of reliable communications that is difficult."

"Ok, thanks Stacy. Keep me informed of your progress on a daily basis. We have to get things more back to normal." The President looks around the table and focuses on the Director of National Intelligence.

"What about Kim?"

The DNI stands to his full 6'6" height. "Mr. President, we have a company of Marines approaching the secret Site 357. We are taking extreme precautions in the event it's a trap. But we are ninety percent confident that the two Generals will hand over Kim within the next several hours."

"Excellent. At that point how quickly can we declare the war over?"

General Seibert stands. "Mr. President if General Ri and General Jeong are telling us the truth. They should be able to communicate with their staffs to bring about a cease fire within a day or two."

"Good, that will save thousands of lives on both sides."

Again the President scans the faces of those seated with him until he settles on the faces of his two most ardent critics. "Senator, I'd like to get the Congress back to work as quickly as possible. So I've authorized the military to transport each member of the House and each Senator from the Greenbrier to their office or their homes."

Senator Claiborne smiles. "Thank you Mr. President. I know that on the Senate side, we are anxious to help to bring the country back from this devastating attack. But I am troubled by the sneak attack by North Korea and Iran and why the intelligence agencies did not alert you and Congress of the presence of nuclear weapons in the hands of our two enemies."

George Watkins is less civil. "Mr. President, did you have any prior knowledge of the potential attack? If so, then you failed to protect the American people."

The President is not surprised by both men being critical of him, but he is surprised at the direct accusations. "Gentlemen, I am not going to discuss this situation while we are still dealing with the Iranians and the North Koreans. At the appropriate time, I will address your questions. Thank you all for your hard work."

With that, the President rises and leaves the room. Trailing him is his Chief of Staff with a smile on his face.

Chapter 46

Los Angeles, CA
September 11th

Jennifer and Mary have eaten their last can of soup for breakfast. Jennifer is now starting to get nervous that they will run out of food before the crisis ends. She walks into the pantry and sees two packages of noodles, three cans of tuna, one bag of rice, a half empty jar of peanut butter and a large bag of Nestlé's chocolate chips.

Suddenly Mary is at her side. "There is someone at the front door knocking."

Jennifer walks out of the pantry and can now hear the knocking. Mary grabs her gun and follows her mother through the dining room and into the front hallway. They both freeze and listen.

"Jennifer, its Dominick. I just wanted to check on you and Mary."

Mary looks at her mother. "Maybe he has some food?" She whispers.

Jennifer moves to the door, "Hi Dominick. We are ok."

"Ok, good. Hey listen, I have some extra food that I'd like to trade for any alcohol you don't want. Abby is out of her stash and I am concerned about her."

Jennifer moves to the side window that looks onto the front steps. What she can see is her neighbor holding a large box that she assumes contains the food. She has to make a quick decision. "Ok, we have to remove a barrier."

Jennifer moves to Mary's side. "Put the gun away but keep it close. Go find all the bottles of alcohol, but keep back a couple of the vodka for trade later."

As Mary goes to the bar to collect the bottles, Jennifer dislodges the 2x4 piece

288

of lumber. She unlocks the front door and swings it open. With a staged smile she says, "Hi Dominick, how are you guys doing?"

Dominick smiles and steps inside. "We are doing ok. We went to the store just a day before the EMPs and we have plenty. But Abby has gone through her booze and I am concerned about her if she isn't drinking. She goes into fits of rage and I am concerned she might hurt herself."

Jennifer knows about alcoholism and how they spiral downward with or without their drink of choice. "I am sorry to hear about that. I think we have some alcohol I can give you."

At that point, Mary walks into the hallway carrying a box full of bottles. "I don't know what she drinks, but there is an assortment here."

Jennifer can see Dominick's face change when he sees Mary. Jennifer looks at her daughter and for the first time notices her womanly body. She is wearing a pair of cutoff jeans that are a bit too high showing off her tan thighs and a t-shirt without a bra that shows off her pert breasts. As Mary bends to put the box down, Dominick gets a nice view of her full breasts.

"What do you have to trade?" Jennifer says to try to distract the neighbor.

Dominick's eyes shift to Jennifer and he smiles. "I have ten cans of soup, six cans of salmon, two cans of pork-n-beans, a bag of potatoes, a bag of onions and three bags of cookies. What do you need?"

Jennifer looks into the box. "We have enough food for another week or so. This would definitely help. Thanks for thinking of us."

Suddenly his eyes move up the stairs beyond Jennifer. "What happened there?"

Jihadi White Christmas

Jennifer turns and sees the blood from the intruder that they tried to clean up. Three of the stairs have blood stains that they were unable to get out.

"Mark had an accident a month or so ago and cut his leg. He bled all over the house." Jennifer says with a smile. "That was one area we couldn't clean up. We were planning to replace all the carpeting anyway."

Dominick's eyes travel from Jennifer to Mary who is standing several yards away. "Ok, well thanks for the booze. That should keep Judy sauced for a week or so. That will keep her off my back."

Jennifer forces a weak smile.

The neighbor picks up the box then turns to Jennifer. "Any idea when they might turn on the electricity? I heard that the military is delivering food and water to distribution centers downtown. Do you want to drive down with me to check it out?"

Jennifer shakes her head. "I think it's still too dangerous to venture out. I have no idea when the lights might come on."

"Ok, well, I'll check on you guys again in a couple of days." Dominick says with a smile towards Mary.

As he leaves, Jennifer closes and locks the door, then wedges the 2x4 between the stairs and the door.

"God, what a creep." Says Mary.

"We have to be careful since he now knows how we are securing the front door. I don't trust him." Jennifer explains.

"Well he doesn't know I have this." As Mary pulls the 9mm from the small of her back.

"Hopefully you won't have to use it. But we can't trust anyone at this point.

Jihadi White Christmas

Let's check out the food and please put on
a bra."

Chapter 47

Anju, North Korea
September 11th

The North Korea Special Forces have been told that the war is over and that they are not to fire on any American or South Korean forces.

General Ri is standing outside the gates of site 357 as the American troops approach with caution. He was alerted to their presence by the sensors placed strategically around the facility. The General has his sidearm but otherwise he is at their mercy.

As the Americans walk within a few yards, the General bows. "My name is General Ri. I have been in contact with President Baker regarding the transfer of Chairman Kim to your custody."

294

The Army Ranger Major salutes. "My name is Major Charles Irish. I have been told to take custody of the Chairman and transport him back to Pyongyang for questioning. I would ask that you and General Jeong accompany us for your safety."

The General is pleased. "Yes of course. I have issued a formal communication to all of our armed forces that the North Korean government has agreed to a cease fire and all personnel should lay down their arms and surrender to the Americans."

"Thank you General. Your troops and your people will be treated with respect and given food and water. Now we would like to see Chairman Kim and transport him to one of our vehicles."

The General nods, and then offers the Major his sidearm. The Major accepts the revolver and hands it to a sergeant. As the men walk through the gates, the Green Berets disarm each guard and sits them in a line. They take the elevator down into the control room and as they disembark Major Irish sees several dozen North Korean soldiers standing at attention.

The Major salutes and the General tells them in Korean to stand at ease. Then General Ri introduces General Jeong and they shake hands. The three walk down a long hallway to a room on their left. There are two guards standing at attention. The General produces a key and unlocks the door.

As they enter the room, the Major sees a form on a bed. The lights are low and standing next to the bed is an older man.

"Major Irish, this is Doctor Seong, who has been instrumental in keeping the Chairman sedated."

The Major nods towards the doctor and says, "What is his condition now?"

The doctor looks at his notes. "The Chairman is resting comfortably. His respiration is normal. His blood pressure is 150/90. Too high but considering his weight and the circumstances, it is acceptable. He can travel if that is your question."

The Major nods. "Excellent. We would like to get him to Pyongyang as soon as possible. If we can get the Chairman to declare the end of the war, then millions of people will be saved."

"He can be ready to be transported within the next ten minutes."

The Major turns to his second in command. "Sergeant, accompany the doctor and the Chairman to the surface and place them in the Stryker Armored Vehicle."

"Yes sir!"

The trio exits the room and head for the surface. Upon reaching the front gate, the Major calls for his communications officer. "Set up a call with command. Let them know we have package number one secured and will return to headquarters as soon as we can. Also let them know we have the packages two and three." Indicating the two Generals.

"Yes sir!"

The Rangers secure Site 357 with several hundred Special Forces troops. This operation has been successful and thousands of lives on both sides will be saved. With America's help, hopefully a reunified Korea will heal and become an economic powerhouse, and Kim Jong-Un will pay for his actions over the past ten years.

Chapter 48

Washington D.C.
September 11th

Senator Jordan Claiborne is sitting in his large office in the Hart Senate Office Building. In his inner office, he is having a second stiff drink. Within the next ten minutes the Speaker of the House will meet with him to discuss their Black Flag operation.

Once they authorize the operation, there is no going back. If caught they will face treason charges. If they don't move forward, then the CABAL will eliminate them both and their families. He is 78 years old, too old and not interested in the stresses of the Presidency. But he knows that the Speaker wants the position and the power.

He is relatively young at 63 and serving two Presidential terms would not be an issue.

"The Senator hears his phone buzz. "Yes Carol."

"Senator, the Speaker is here to see you."

"Yes, please show him in."

The outer door opens and Speaker Watkins strides into the Senator's office with a grim look on his face.

"Good afternoon George."

George Watkins sits in a chair opposite the Senator. "Jordan, we have to accelerate the Black Flag protocol."

"Why? What's happened?"

"You saw in the Cabinet meeting that the President didn't take the bait to declare Martial Law. He put the decision off for a few days. Also, I heard from Randy Smith that the military just captured Kim and the President is about to declare the end of the war against North Korea."

The Senator considers this new information. "That will make things more difficult."

Watkins gets up and helps himself to a drink from the Senator's in-office bar. "There are two major issues; one is who will do the hit. The second is that we have to eliminate both the President and the Vice President in the same event."

Senator Claiborne nods. "What would you suggest?"

"There are only several events that would bring the President and Vice President into the same room. We'll have to have a bomb placed in the Oval Office or the Cabinet room. Then there is who will place the bomb?"

The two men sit silently sipping their drinks considering their options.

"Randy Smith has been very helpful; he wants to sit in your seat Senator."

The Senator chuckles. "Well, we can use that to get him to help us. If he does this, he can have my seat. I'll work with him to make sure he is elected."

"Ok, I know a guy who can build a bomb for us that will destroy a room of that size. Randy can place the bomb in his briefcase right behind the President and Vice President. The Secret Service won't think someone that close to the President will want him dead." Says the Speaker.

Jordan takes another sip then says, "Ok let's get it done soon. Within the next week, no later. Can we make it look like an Al-Qaeda attack?"

The Speaker considers the suggestion. "You know Michelle Samaha is Muslim. We could frame her and make sure she is there."

"Excellent. She is part of the President's black project. It's illegal and will give us justification to shut that program

302

down." The Senator finishes his drink. "With you as the new President, we'll be able to restructure the government in our image making sure both parties maintain their power for the next hundred years."

George Watkins smiles. He has been seeking the ultimate political prize over the last thirty years. Suddenly, it is within his grasp. President Watkins sounds just right.

Chapter 49

The Ramsar Parsian Hotel
September 12th

Mark and Michelle received a note from the Supreme Leader asking them to stay at the hotel for a day and then his office will send some people to escort them to the Presidential Palace tomorrow. They get room service and go for a swim in the Caspian Sea.

While walking on the beach Mark and Michelle discuss the attack on the Iranian leadership. "Your briefcase has the VX gas in a canister. With just six ounces, the release will kill everyone in that room within seconds. If they scan your briefcase it will not show up, it is built into the frame. The trigger is on the handle. After the case is armed, you just have to press the
304

handle down and the timer will start. You will have thirty seconds to get out of the room."

Mark nods. "I have heard of VX gas but what are the effects?"

Michelle searches her memory for information on VX. "It is an organophosphorus compound. It's a nerve agent that is odorless and tasteless. Within seconds of release, the subjects will feel tightness in the chest, there will be muscle spasms, then death by asphyxiation or a heart attack. It will be over very quickly."

"What about our escape?"

Michelle reviews the plan in her head. "There will be two armed guards at the door. I and the four SEALs will be seated outside the conference room. There is a secretary who controls the conference room schedule. You will be the only one in the room to give your presentation on their financials. Exactly at 3:12 pm, your watch will give you a silent buzz. The briefcase timer will count down thirty seconds. You will then make an excuse to leave the room. At the same time Kelly Campos will call the Secretary and play a recording of the Supreme Leader telling the secretary to lock the conference room and that they are not to be disturbed for the next three hours."

"How did you get that recording?"

Kelly Campos recorded the Supreme Leader talking on his phone or in meetings over the past two weeks. Most of it was administrative, but we used the computer to put together a string of words that says what we want him to say. The secretary of course knows the Supreme Leaders voice, so we couldn't use a translator. As you leave the meeting, she will assume they want to discuss what you told them and she will lock the door and give us a three hour window to get back to the beach in the limo and back inside Proteus."

306

Jihadi White Christmas

"Ok, what is plan two if the secretary or someone else wants to enter the room?"

Michelle shrugs. "I guess we use the weapons stashed in the limo and shoot our way back to the beach."

Mark smiles. "Ok, either way I want to make sure that the Supreme Leader, the President and General Aziz die. If that doesn't happen, then I doubt The Green Revolution will succeed."

Michelle turns up from the beach heading for the hotel. "They are ready to flood into the streets to call for a new government. If we are successful; they will have hundreds of thousands of women, students, labor and the middle class protestors marching in the streets. At that point, it will be up to the people of Iran. Tomorrow we'll know."

Chapter 50

Washington D.C.
September 12th

The President is sitting in the Oval Office reading a report on the percentage of the country that has electrical service. In the West, it's fifty-eight percent. In the South, almost forty percent and in the Midwest/NE it's twenty-two percent. More and more communities are getting their lights on. Within just three weeks, America has not only survived a nuclear attack, but has started the long road toward normalization. It's been remarkable.

The President puts down the report. "Damn, this is good news." He says to Randy Smith.

"Yes sir. But there are many other issues that we have to deal with."

The President looks up, "of course, but the EMPs could have crippled the country for months or years. What is happening with a national television speech?"

The Chief of Staff shifts from one foot to another. "I am talking with the big three to figure out when they will be ready for your address. Maybe by the end of the week."

The President picks up another report. "Well, the sooner the better."

"Yes sir. Oh, another issue. The Vice President has suggested that the two of you meet with the Cabinet members perhaps in Cabinet room to talk about the good news and have that exchange recorded that can then be broadcast at a later date. It would be good PR."

The President is engrossed in the report detailing food and water distribution, only half listening. "Ok, sounds good. Set it up."

Randy Smith smiles. "Yes sir."

As the Chief of Staff leaves the Oval Office, the President's secretary sticks her head in. "Mr. President, I have General Seibert on line one."

The President sits forward and pushes the conference call button for line one. "Yes General."

"Mr. President I am happy to report that Chairman Kim has been secured and is currently being transported to South Korea. Within a couple of hours, we will issue a communication to the people of North Korea that the war is over and will show the Chairman shackled. General Ri and General Jeong will address the nation asking all of the North Korean people to cooperate with the American forces for the good of the country."

"Excellent. Once that has happened, I'll make sure I include that in my address to the American people as soon as it can be arranged."

"Also sir, the Iranian operation has been delayed one day. We expect that tomorrow we should know about their success by the end of the day."

"Ok, is the delay an issue?"

"No sir, the delay was at the behest of the Iranian leadership. Everything is still on schedule."

The President considers that new information. "Ok, keep me informed of any issues. After all that has happened over the past several weeks, this good news will do a lot to raise the morale of the American people."

Chapter 51

S-Cubed Headquarters
September 13th

Kelly Campos has been at his workstation for the past twelve hours. He has been monitoring the communications between the various leaders in Iran. He has been piecing together multiple conversations that is starting to reveal the mosaic of a sinister plan by General Aziz and his son. Suddenly Kelly is aware of someone sitting on the floor to his left. He turns in his swivel chair and sees the new girl watching him.

"You shouldn't be here."

"Why not? Are you working on secret stuff?"

Kelly smiles. "Yeah, secret agent type stuff."

"So what are you doing?"

Kelly considers whether he can tell her anything about his job or what information he has at his finger tips. She is very cute and has a great smile. "Ok, I use the computer to translate conversations and try to figure out what the bad guys are planning."

Kristen looks at Kelly for several seconds, and then says "So your last name is Campos? You are Latino?"

Kelly smiles. "Well, my father was from Mexico. He went to college in England and met my mother there. She was from Ireland. Her name is Aoife." He says with a twinkle in his eyes.

"Ocoffee? What kind of name is that?"

Kelly laughs. "It's Gaelic. It's an Irish name that means beauty or radiance. But everyone calls her Eva."

"Ah, that is something I can remember."

"So my dad's name was Hector Campos. My mom's name is Aoife O'Brien. I was born two years after they were married just after they moved to the Boston area. Therefore, I am Kelly Campos. I'm a combination of both cultures."

"Nice. So how did you get this job?"

Kelly laughs. "Well, it's a long story but the bottom line is that while I was at M.I.T. I embezzled several million dollars using a computer algorithm that I wrote to transfer a few cents of every Bank of North Boston transaction to an off-shore account. Then I would give away tens or hundreds of thousands of dollars to various charities."

"You didn't take any of the money yourself?"

"Nah, I didn't need money. I had a full ride scholarship at M.I.T. and my mom is fairly well off. So it was more of a Robin Hood idea."

Kristen smiles. "Wow, very, very cool."

"Well, not that cool. It got me kicked out of school and I almost went to prison for ten years. But Michelle gave me a second chance, and I won't let her down."

"Nice! My mom and dad are both from Guatemala. I am the fourth of six children. Unfortunately my brothers got into gangs. Two are in jail and my older brother was killed when they tried to hold up the cop and the guy with the motorcycle."

"That guy on the motorcycle is Ducky Duckworth. He is a warrior. You are lucky he didn't shoot you too."

"I know. I didn't think the gang would pull their guns. But when they did everything happened so fast. I just froze."

Suddenly Kelly's computer dings. Kelly swings back to his workstation and keys in a few words. He whistles.

"What is it?" asks Kristen.

"Something I have to check out and something you don't need to know."

"Can I just stay and watch you work? I am really, really bored up in that office."

Kelly smiles. "Sure. Just sit over on the couch over there. I have several books I am reading. Hope you like science fiction."

Kristen gets up from the floor. "Sure, I love to read just about anything."

Kelly's attention is drawn back to his computer screen.

"So you live down here?"

Absentmindedly he responds. "Yep, I brought in a bed and a refrigerator and it allows me to stay here 24/7."

"Cool. Is there a shower down here?"

"There is a full gym and showers just down the hallway. Before the EMP I was able to order food, but now we have a full cafeteria where we can get any kind of food. Plus there is a small movie theatre down here too."

"Wow, this is much better than where I was living. I could stay here for years."

Kelly laughs and looks over. "I won't go that far, but it is safe and we can ride out the EMP here."

Although there is only three years of age difference between them, Kelly is fairly naive regarding the female species and doesn't pick up on any of Kristen's cues. Whereas Kristen is mature beyond her years and is already thinking of her future with this big lovable guy.

Chapter 52

The Ramsar Parsian Hotel
September 13th

Mark and Michelle last night were very aware that they were together in a hotel and their feelings could get in the way of their mission. After taking their showers, they agreed to sleep in separate rooms. Their two bedroom *Presidential* suite was very opulent and afforded them a luxurious and much needed sleep.

Mark was up at dawn and went for a run. When he came back at first light, Michelle was standing in a robe on the balcony with a cup of coffee. Mark comes up from behind her and slowly wraps his arms around her. Mark kisses the back of her neck. "Good morning."

Jihadi White Christmas

Michelle can feel a heat rising throughout her body. She smiles and replies huskily. "Good morning. We have fresh coffee on the credenza."

Mark takes the hint and moves to grab a cup of strong coffee. On a tray are several rolls, some jam and several pieces of fruit.

They both know that today is a big day. They could both be dead in several hours. Carrying a banana, Mark peels it and takes a big bite. Moving onto the balcony where he is sure there are no listening devices. He whispers to Michelle. "The Quds guys will be here at 10 am. They will want us to get into their vehicle. I will refuse and insist that we take the limo. That will enable our SEALs to be with us, but also ensure our ride is at the site to take us out of there."

Michelle can feel his body slightly pressing into her. She smiles and looks up

319

at him. "Good plan. What do you want me to do?"

Mark can feel his excitement rising and tries to distract himself. "Just be your beautiful self and keep me informed of anything unusual happening outside the conference room. I'll have my earpiece in."

Each of the team members will have custom made wireless tactical communications devices that fit inside their ear. It will allow Michelle to communicate with Mark and all of the team members. Since Michelle will be wearing a scarf, she can hide her mic and power source.

Michelle nods.

Suddenly Michelle's secure cellular phone buzzes. Michelle moves to a table and picks it up. She sees that it is Kelly.

"Yes Kelly."

"Good morning Michelle. I know its early but I have some very interesting information."

Michelle knows this is an encrypted phone and anything they say will stay between them. "What is it?"

Kelly takes a breath. "I just translated a conversation between Aziz and his son. It seems like they are planning a coup. I was not able to get all of the details, but I think it's imminent. I'll keep digging."

Michelle considers this new bit of information. "Text me what he said and also the Farsi full text. I might be able to translate it and get more detail."

"Will do."

"How is it going there Kelly?"

"Excellent. We are safe and hoping your operation is successful. If there is anything you need from here, just let me know."

"Ok, we leave in about two hours. If we need any help, I'll text you."

After hanging up, she turns to Mark on the balcony and whispers. "Seems Aziz has plans of his own. Kelly intercepted a conversation with his son about a coup."

Mark raises his eye brows. "When?"

"Kelly thinks it during your presentation. The Quds force in the room will start shooting at some point or a bomb has been placed. Probably after Aziz leaves on some pretext they plan to eliminate the leadership. If he leaves the room, you need to leave also."

Mark considers the information. "Then perhaps we don't have to use the VX?"

Michelle nods. "Kelly is trying to get more information, I'll pass it on to you if he comes up with something more."

Mark smiles. "You are the most intelligent person I know. You'll figure it out. Hopefully it will be in time."

Chapter 53

Washington D.C.
September 13th

Randy Smith knows he is walking a dangerous path. He is ambitious, he always has been. When in high school he put castor oil in a rival's hot chocolate just before they took their final exam. Randy got the highest grades and the title valedictorian, while his rival sat on the toilet and emptied his bowels unable to finish the AP tests. In college at Harvard, he paid a friend who worked in the computer center to doctor his grades on two classes he almost failed. Instantly he received an A on both classes and qualified for an internship with one of the state Senators. That launched him on his career and to this particular point.

He is meeting with a real bomb maker. Randy can't believe he is doing this, but with a Senate seat on the line he would do anything.

The building he approaches is in a commercial area, indistinct from any of the others nearby. He walks up to the front door and sees two cameras watching him from two different angles. Randy tries the door but knows in the back of his mind that it's locked. Suddenly a voice on a speaker says, "Can I help you?"

Randy looks up at one of the cameras and says, "I am here to see Mickey."

There is a slight pause. "What is the code word?"

Randy had been briefed that the security would be extensive and that if questioned he was given a one word response. "Mantle".

Jihadi White Christmas

The door is unlocked and Randy pulls it open and steps inside. Once he is in the reception area, he hears the door locked behind him. A door in front of him unlocks and Randy steps inside a large warehouse. In the center of the room, Randy sees a single table lit by two floodlights. As he walks towards the table he sees a figure in an all white clean room suit. The man steps away from the table and removes the mask and then takes off the disposable bunny suit but keeps on his disposable gloves. The person that emerges is in his mid-60s, white hair and a bushy beard. He smiles. "It pays to be careful. The FBI has amazing technical capabilities to recover any DNA left on the device even after it explodes. The man hands Randy a pair of flesh colored disposable gloves. "You should put these on and wear gloves when handling the briefcase."

Randy nods as he pulls on the plastic gloves.

"The blast radius will be 100 yards. Inside a closed room, every person there will be killed. No question. I have put it inside this briefcase. I have a timing device inside that can be set by pushing this button. It will give you the ten minutes to leave that you asked for."

"Can the bomb detonate without pushing the button?"

"No, the button connects the circuit and starts the clock countdown."

"If the button is pushed accidentally can the countdown be stopped?"

"No. Once it's pushed you have ten minutes before the explosion."

Randy considers this. "Ok. I'll make sure everything is in place before I push the button."

The bomb maker nods. He picks up the briefcase and hands it to Randy. He

Jihadi White Christmas

then walks Randy to the door. "By the way,
we never met, I don't know you and you
don't know me. If you violate that trust,
you will wish you went up with the bomb."

Chapter 54

Tehran Iran
September 13th

As predicted, the Quds soldiers requested
that Mark and Michelle travel with them in
their military vehicle. But Mark declined
and insisted that he travel in the Limousine
with his guards. Two Quds followed the
Limo, while two in a second vehicle lead in
their drive to Tehran. The meeting was
scheduled for 1 pm at the exclusive
Sa'dabad Complex. It is located on 300
hectares built by the Qajar and Pahlavi
monarchs in the 19th Century. After the
1979 Cultural Revolution it was converted to
a museum. The museum has been closed
for the past several days as security was
increased to allow the Supreme Leader, the
President of Iran, the top military leader,

and most of the Mullahs to meet with their financial advisor. Security is tight.

As the limousine arrives, General Aziz and his son walk down the stone stairs to greet this guest. None of the Iranians have met Peter Monterie of the Habib Banque Zurich, but he was highly recommended as a banker that can realize high rates of returns for investments. He only deals with customers with millions to invest. Over the past thirty years the Iranian leadership has stolen Billions from the treasury and invested in secure Swiss banks.

Two years ago, as Peter Monterie suggested the Iranian President and the Mullahs developed a strategy to invest in gold. As world events get more and more unstable, the price of gold goes up. If a war breaks out or if the Great Satan suffers a devastating attack, then the price of gold will soar. Over the past several weeks with the invasion of North Korea, the missile attack and the EMPs, the price of gold has reached beyond anyone's expectations.

Now that America has been hit with three EMPs, the Iran leadership is excited to find out how much their investments have risen.

Mark exits the limo and extends his hand to his wife while Aziz and his son wait. This irritates Aziz as women are second class citizens in Iran and the banker should have met with them first, then helped his wife. The four guards also exit the limo and form a protective semi-circle around the couple. At this point Mark turns his attention to Aziz. "Good afternoon General Aziz. As you know I am Peter Monterie, this is my wife Michelle."

Aziz turns his fake smile and shifts his gaze to the banker's wife. She is wearing a scarf and a long dress covering her legs and arms, but Aziz can see that she is beautiful. He breaks into a big smile. "Mrs. Monterie, I am pleased to meet you." Giving Michelle a low bow.

Michelle smiles and nods but does not shake his hand. That would be forbidden in a Muslim country.

The group enters the Sa'dabad Complex and walks down a long marble hallway. Mark along side Aziz, with Michelle trailing several yards behind. Ducky and the three SEALs walking closely behind the group take in every room and person along the walkway. It is obvious that there is high level leadership in the building. Every hundred yards there are several Quds military armed with automatic weapons, standing at attention.

As they come to several large wooden doors, Aziz turns to Michelle and the guards and tells them they can sit on the benches opposite the conference room. Michelle smiles and walks slowly to the bench and sits. Her guards stand on either side.

Suddenly a young man exits the conference room and approaches Aziz. He snaps off a smart salute and says, "General, all of the guests are in the room and it has been swept for explosives. The meeting is ready to begin."

General Aziz smiles. "Mr. Monterie I would like to introduce you to my son, Captain Sajad Aziz."

Mark can feel his blood run cold as he looks upon his sister's husband. If it wasn't for the lives of Michelle and the Navy SEALs, he would have leapt upon him and killed him with his own bare hands. But the operation is most important now, revenge should be put on the back burner.

Mark extends his hand and smiles. "Good afternoon Captain. Very nice to meet you."

Jihadi White Christmas

After the two shake hands, Mark is led into the conference room carrying his brief case containing of his presentation and the deadly VX gas.

Chapter 55

Washington D.C.
September 13th

Randy Smith is sitting in his office thinking about what he is about to do and his future. As Chief of Staff, he has full access to the President and Vice President and he has the power to call meetings or influence people. But he wants more power and more influence. But being a Senator and only one of one hundred people that wield more power than the American public knows, that is his ultimate goal. He thought he had latched onto a rising star with President Baker. An independent who had a long shot to win the Presidency, but he did win overcoming both major political parties. But it is clear that the President can not be influenced and is unwilling to play the political game.

When the Speaker of the House contacted him for a secret meeting, Randy was surprised. They met at a cabin in rural Northern Virginia. When Randy arrived, he passed through the security parameter of the Speaker's guards, and then was shown into the main room where he found one of the most powerful men sitting in a comfortable chair sipping a drink. The discussion was short and one sided. The Speaker outlined the plan and secured Randy's agreement to place the bomb.

Randy smiles thinking about placing the blame for the assassination of the President and Vice President on Michelle Samaha. She has been the favorite of the President and Randy thinks she is potentially a traitor. Randy doesn't trust any Muslim and especially Michelle Samaha.

Randy picks up his phone and tells his secretary that the President wants to have a Cabinet meeting and to include the Vice President in four days. Set the schedule.

As he puts down the phone he takes a deep breath. This is a huge gamble but with an even bigger payoff. His plan is starting to come together, now he just has to execute.

Chapter 56

Los Angeles, CA
September 13th

Their Post-EMP life has settled into a steady rhythm. With no television, no radio, no internet and no cellular service, suddenly Mary is thrust back into the middle ages according to her. She is laying on a lounge chair next to their pool sunning herself on a bright warm September day. Jennifer is laying down trying to get some rest after staying up most of the night guarding the downstairs area.

Mary is reading a book that her mom suggested. It's a soapy romance novel, but Mary has been drawn into the story. Suddenly she has the feeling of being watched. She puts the book down and slowly turns her head. Out of the

337

corner of her eye she sees a man standing in their yard by the gate.

"Hi Mary, how are you doing?"

Mary turns suddenly and jumps up and sees its her creepy neighbor Dominick. "What are you doing back here?"

Dominick smiles and steps forward. He is wearing a LA Dodgers t-shirt and a pair of kaki shorts. "I knocked on the front door but nobody answered. I have some additional food you might be craving."

Mary is suddenly aware of what she is wearing. A string bikini. She can see that her neighbor is taking it all in. He smiles. "You'll have to talk with my mom."

Dominick nods. "Where is your mom?"

Mary starts to back up. She now wishes she had brought her gun with her. But when she came out to sun herself, she put it on the kitchen table when she grabbed a towel to lay on. "She is in the kitchen, I'll go get her."

As Mary starts towards the kitchen, Dominick puts his arm out barring her way. She can feel his hand on her shoulder, his forearm touching her breasts. She stops froze in fear. She looks up and sees his eyes focused on her cleavage.

"Mary, maybe you and I can come to an agreement." She sees the sneer on his lips. "I can protect you, keep you from getting hurt with all this mess. Who knows how long this will last, could be months or even years before the government gets it's head out of its ass. There are a lot roving gangs out there that would hurt you, I can protect you. I have several guns."

Dominick has now moved closer and is pressing his large bulk against Mary. He outweighs her probably by 150 lbs. "Come on Mary, play ball with me. Your mom doesn't need to know."

As Dominick moves behind Mary she prepares to bolt to the kitchen door. Then Dominick's thick right arm moves up to around her neck pinning her to his body. She can feel his erection against her and she feels like she is going to throw up. His hand moves down and slides inside her swim top. Mary wants to scream, but she can't seem to get it out. "Come on baby, I can help you. Let's go over to my house."

He starts to move her slowly across their patio towards the gate. Mary knows that if this monster can get her into his house, she will be raped and probably killed at some point.

Mary starts to struggle, but Dominick grabs her mouth with his other hand and lifts her off the ground. Panic sets in and Mary starts to kick wildly. As they approach the gate, they hear a voice.

"Put her down or I'll blow your head off."

Dominick stops. He slowly turns and sees Jennifer standing about ten feet away pointing Mary's 9mm.

He partially releases Mary and smiles. "Hey, I was just joking around. No harm, no foul right?"

Jennifer hasn't moved. Dominick has kept his hand on Mary's shoulder to keep her in front of him. "Let her go or I will shoot."

Dominick smiles again. "No you won't. I know you are anti-gun, you had a lawn sign against the NRA last year. But I can see that you still have the safety on."

With that, Dominick throws Mary to the side and bull rushes Jennifer pulling his own gun from behind his back. Two gun shots ring out. Both shots hit their target. Jennifer deftly steps to the side as Dominick's large bulk goes into motion, it stays in motion. The first shot hit the man in the stomach, the second hit his heart.

Jennifer and Mary watch as Dominick falls and hits the pool deck, then splashes into the water. Jennifer keeps the gun trained on his back as he floats. She is sure at some point he will magically leapt out of the pool and attack her and her daughter.

They see a blood stain spreading through the water, Dominick's body facedown starts to sink.

Jennifer starts to shake, and then she feels her daughter's hand taking the gun from her hands. "Its OK mom, you did the right thing. He was going to rape and kill me."

Jennifer pulls her daughter into her arms and they both start to cry. After a few minutes, Jennifer takes a deep breath. "I guess we need to get him out of the pool and bury him with the others."

Chapter 57

Tehran, Iran
September 14th

Just as Mark is about to enter the conference room with Aziz, he turns and smiles at Michelle. She returns his smile knowing that this could be the last time they see each other. After Mark disappears into the room, Michelle sits on a couch opposite to wait.

"Ducky, would you go down to the Limo and wait there for us. Make sure everything is ready to go." Michelle whispers.

Ducky nods and walks purposely down the hall towards the outside doors.

Inside the room, Mark is greeted by twelve of the most powerful men in Iran. The Supreme leader is sitting at the head of the table. His Mullahs are spread around the table as are several military leaders.

Mark introduces himself to each in French, then moves to the projector and puts his briefcase on the table. He opens it pulls out his presentation. He closes the briefcase but he doesn't hit the button to start the timer. He knows the Quds force may start shooting shortly and he only has minutes to get out of the room.

Mark glances around the room and notes four Quds with AK-47s standing at attention but looking towards their Sergeant Each has a silencer on their AK-47s. Notes Mark.

General Aziz stands and starts his introduction. "Peter Monterie has managed our Swiss bank accounts for Habib Banque Zurich. Over the past ten years we have made excellent returns but now with the meteoric rise in the price of gold Mr. Monterie felt it was important to give us an accounting of our returns and be available to answer any questions you might have."

At that point, Aziz's cellular phone rings. The General looks at the caller and frowns. "I am sorry, I have an urgent call. Mr. Monterie, would you please start with your presentation?"

With that, General Aziz leaves the room. Mark now realizes that the coup will start in this room. He understands that the loyal Quds will start shooting at anytime.

After Aziz leaves, Mark smiles and says, "I must also excuse myself, I forgot to get the copies of each of your accounts for you to review. I will be right back."

Mark turns and grabs his briefcase and heads for the door while the surprised Supreme Leader and Mullahs look on. Mark exits the conference room and nods to Michelle. Michelle says a code word to Kelly Campos, who then calls to the secretary seated just outside the two large doors.

The secretary answers her phone and hears the Supreme leaders voice. "no one is to enter the conference room for the next three hours." The phone call is ended and the secretary reaches under her desk to lock the doors.

Michelle rises as she sees Mark exit the conference room. The group then quickly walks down the hallway and out to their waiting limousine.

As the limo leaves the compound Mark sees another car ahead of them speeding towards the main highway. Mark leans forward and says to the driver; "Catch that car if you can."

Mark turns to Michelle. "I think that is General Aziz and his son."

As the two cars speed onto the main highway, the SEALs pull their weapons. "Cut them off if you can, then assault the car", Mark says.

Jihadi White Christmas

As the limousine accelerates to catch up to the SUV, someone leans out of the vehicle and fires two shots into the limo windshield.

The Mossad driver evades and pulls behind the SUV limiting their shooting angle.

Mark considers the situation. "Pull up next to them, everyone get down."

The limo accelerates while Mark grabs his briefcase. He rolls down his window and ducks while the General fires his revolver into the open window. Mark counts each shot, then when there is a pause Mark pushes the button on his briefcase and lends out, then throws it into the SUV. "Go, Go, Go!" Mark yells to the Limo driver.

The limousine accelerates while the SUV slows down. While Mark watches, the car then runs off the side of the road and rolls to a stop.

"Should we go back to make sure they are dead?" Says Michelle.

"No, the VX gas could still be in the car and just a whiff of it could kill us. Let's get to the coast and out of here before they figure out what happened." Replies Mark.

The limo heads north and the extraction by the Proteus mini-sub.

Chapter 58

Washington D.C.
September 14th

The President is sitting behind the Resolute desk in the Oval Office waiting for the radio microphone to turn on. His speech to the nation is being broadcasted via radio since none of the television channels are operational yet. He has been told that in many parts of the country CB radios and solar powered radios will be able to pick up the broadcast.

The Chief of Staff, Randy Smith is pacing behind the technicians and staff members.

"Randy, stop pacing. What is wrong?"

"Nothing sir. Just a lot on my plate."

349

The President looks up from his notes. "Well, get it together. There is still a lot to do."

With that, the Communications Director moves to the President and tells him that they will go live in thirty seconds.

The President sits up straighter and looks over this prepared speech. The Communications Director holds up five fingers, then four, then three and then points to the President.

"My fellow Americans. Over the past three weeks the United States of America has been attacked by two foreign nations. After North Korea launched ten nuclear tipped ICBMs, the United States declared war. Fortunately all of those ICBMs either failed to launch or were shot down by our defensive systems. Unfortunately, one ICBM shot at Japan did hit Tokyo resulting in several hundred thousands of Japanese citizens being killed or injured in a nuclear attack. American and South Korean forces then launched a counter-attack on North Korea. Within several days, the leader of North Korea Kim Jung-Un was captured and the surrender of North Korea was announced." The President takes a breath.

"However, at the same time, three ICBMs were launched from Southern Syria by Iranian forces using Russian missile technology. Those ICBMs did evade our defensive systems and they detonated two hundred miles above the United States causing an Electro-Magnetic Pulse that has destroyed or damaged many of our electrical components. This attack has shutdown our electrical system nationwide, has stopped delivery of food and water and caused riots in several large cities." Again the President pauses.

"That is the bad news. The good news is that the major companies that service our electrical grid have been quietly reinforcing their systems over the past decade in anticipation of such an event. Several of the regional grids have been able to get up and operational, most of the others will be operational within the next thirty days. There still may be outages as the system goes to live, but generally the American electrical grid will be fully operational by Thanksgiving."

The President pauses again and then continues. "The U.S. military and reserves have been distributing food and water to many of the large cities and will start focusing on mid-sized cities by next week. We hope to have normal communications systems including the internet up and working by Christmas. This has been an attempt by our enemies to destroy America. They have failed. We will respond appropriately to the Iranian leadership."

Again the President pauses. "I want to thank the American people for being patient, observing our laws and keeping the faith in your government. I will give a weekly address until we determine that the crisis is over. God bless America."

At that point the Communications Director signals to cut the microphone. The President sits back and sighs. He looks up and doesn't see his Chief of Staff.

"Where is Randy?" Asks the President.

Everyone in the room looks around but nobody says anything. "Ok, everyone back to work. Let's right the ship."

Chapter 59

Caspian Sea Coast
September 14th

The limousine is racing the 170 miles from Tehran to the beach near the Ramsar Parsian Hotel where the stash of wetsuits are buried.   As the limo tops the final mountain pass, everyone can see the Caspian Sea and freedom.

It's been almost three hours since the group fled the Presidential Palace and the chaos planned by General Aziz and his son.

"The Quds Force has hopefully completed their mission and killed the Supreme Leader and the Mullahs. Hopefully the Republican Guards are waiting for General Aziz's orders to take over the military." Says Mark.

Michelle nods. "I half expected military helicopters to be looking for us by now. They must suspect we were involved."

Ducky interjects, "In the fog of war you have no idea who is who. You just stick to your mission and let the fog clear."

Mark agrees. "The military is more concerned about a coup, their military leaders are probably searching for Aziz for guidance. But we need to get to the beach as soon as possible and get out to the mini-sub."

It's getting late and the sun is starting to set behind the mountains. The limo speeds down the highway.

As they come around the final curve, they can see the beach to their right and the hotel up on the cliff to their left. The limousine slows at a turnout near the beach and each of the team gets out. Their weapons are left in the limo as they will not be of much use now. The key will be to get through the brush and onto the beach as soon as they can.

Mark exits last and turns to their Mossad driver. "Thank you my friend. Please leave the country as soon as you can. Dispose of the weapons and the limo. They will start looking for us and you as soon as the chaos is sorted out in Tehran." The driver nods and speeds off as Mark closes the door.

The team makes their way into a thicket of bushes where their wetsuits are buried. Each strips out of their business suits and pulls on their wetsuits.

"We need to wait here for a few minutes to make sure the beach is clear. If we are separated, key your watch and swim out as far as you can and wait for the Proteus to pick you up."

Jihadi White Christmas

Suddenly there is a young woman standing at the clearing watching the group. "Are you Americans?" She asks.

Everyone looks towards this girl. Ducky reaches behind his back and grips is 9mm. Mark smiles. "Yes, we are Americans about to go for a swim."

The girl smiles. "Of course and I am the Shah of Iran. On the radio the authorities are looking for six Westerners. I assume that is you?"

Mark steps forward but the girl retreats a step. "We haven't done anything wrong, we just need to get into the water and we'll be gone."

The girl is in a bathing suit and looks to be in her mid-20s. "Can I come with you? I hate what the Mullahs have done to our beautiful country. How they try to control everything we do. I studied English and I will be a good American."

Mark looks at Michelle and she nods. "Ok, you can come with us. We have to get out beyond the surf."

The girl smiles. "Okydoky, Let's go!"

Mark and Michelle smile and follow the girl as she strolls onto the beach. As they start to approach the water, a guard comes out of the deepening gloom.

"Halt, what are you doing?"

Mark stops and turns towards the guard. In French he says, "We are going for a swim."

The guard places his hand on his revolver on his hip. "Speak Farsi."

The girl steps forward and smiles, she says in Farsi. "My father, mother and I are French. We are here on holiday. We are going for a swim."

The guard is surprised, but is taking in the cute figure of the young girl. He is standing facing the trio, but with his hand on his gun.

"How do you know Farsi?"

The girl smiles. "I studied in Tehran for two years. How is my accent?"

The guard smiles back, "It is excellent, but I was told to look out for Westerners."

At that point, after sneaking up behind the guard, Ducky hits the man with the butt of his gun knocking the man out and onto the beach sand. Two of the SEALs race out and grab the man under his arms and pull him into the brush. They tie his arms and legs and stick his sock into his mouth.

Mark, Michelle and their young charge wade into the water. Mark tells them to start swimming and turns to make sure the rest of his team are right behind him. Satisfied that all are in the water, Mark signals for both mini-subs to triangulate on the now seven team members.

After half an hour of steady swimming Mark can see that the girl is tiring quickly. He calls each of the SEALs on their waterproof mics. "Stop swimming, let's wait here for the two Proteus subs."

All of the group form a circle while Mark and Michelle hold the girl above the waves. After ten minutes one of the SEALs feels the Proteus pop up beside him. "Our transportation is here."

Mark pulls the group closer together. "Ducky, you take the SEALs and get into that sub. We'll take the second one."

"No way Mark. You and Michelle and the girl take this one, and we'll wait on the second sub."

Mark hesitates then sees that both Michelle and the girl are barely able to keep their heads about the building surf. "Ok, but we won't leave until the second sub arrives."

Ducky nods and holds the Proteus steady as Mark unlocks the lid and helps Michelle in first, then the Iranian girl. After they are settled, Mark climbs in and Ducky seals the lid.

Just then, the second mini-sub arrives and the SEALs expertly hop in and Ducky seals the lid. "Ok; all of the team is on board, ready to head home."

Mark acknowledges and both subs GPS systems are set for their target pick up spot some 120 miles off the shore. For now they are fairly safe, but unaware if their plan was successful.

Chapter 60

Washington D.C.
September 15th

The Speaker of the House and the Senate Majority leader have returned from the Greenbrier Hotel in West Virginia knowing what is about to happen, they need to be in Washington D.C. to control the aftermath of the assassination.   Both are in their offices alone sipping their favorite drinks trying to steady their nerves.

The Speaker's private phone rings. With the electrical grid in Washington D.C. brought online yesterday, the key political players were the first to get phone service. They are both on secure phones.

"Yes?"

"George, this is Jordan.   Is there anyone there?"

"No, I am alone sitting in my office working on my second drink."

The Senator chuckles. "Yes, me too. Have you heard from Randy?"

They know that the NSA monitors every phone call private or not, and key words are selected by an Artificial Intelligence algorithm. Those calls that are flagged are then reviewed. Neither the Speaker nor the Senator wants the NSA to know of their plans.

"Everything is in place. I spoke with him yesterday and he seems to have the balls to pull this off."

The Senator takes another sip of his special whiskey and sighs. "The meeting should take place within a few days. After that, all hell will break loose for a few weeks or even months. You have to be ready to take control."

The Speaker is the third in line in the event the President and Vice President are unable to fulfill their official duties. Of course after the bomb goes off in the Cabinet room, the speaker will be the last man standing.

"Yes, I know. I have an able staff that will be able to pull the government back together. It won't be easy but its our only shot. Jordan, I'll need your help."

The Senator replies at once. "Of course, of course. I will convene the Senate and we'll pass whatever measures you require to maintain control." He is starting to feel the effects of his second scotch.

The Speaker then smiles to himself. "What about the military? Will they follow new leadership?"

"Absolutely, after an attack by North Korea and Iran? They will be chomping at the bit to kick some ass." Says the Senator. "One major issue might be Mark Aldin, I understand he might be too close to

Samaha." The Senator suddenly realizes that he's said too much.

There is silence on the other end of the phone. Suddenly the Speaker says, "Ok, I think all future communications should be in person. I'll arrange a meeting with your secretary tomorrow. Good night."

The Senator replaces is phone. "Damn." He says to himself. He knows he has to be more careful. The government ears are all around, hopefully the NSA is too busy with other issues to focus on one conversation.

Chapter 61

Baku Azerbaijan
September 16th

The two Proteus mini-subs were picked up by a covert Turkish Navy vessel operating in Azerbaijan waters just off the city of Baku. On board are ten U.S. Navy SEALs at the request of the American President. Relations with Turkey are not always good publically, but militarily they are solid. Turkey understands the military power the U.S. has and they want to maintain their geo-political power in the region, and to do that they need the latest military equipment.

The Turks know that there was a covert U.S. military operation in the area, but didn't know the details. They never would. But when the U.S. President calls the Turkish President asking for their help, things happen.

The seven passengers are then transferred to a helicopter and flown to the city of Kars in Turkey for a U.S. Air Force flight to Greece. After almost twelve hours after leaving Iran, the group is finally out of danger. Once on the U.S. military base in Greece, they are all de-briefed and the Iranian girl is sent to immigration to be processed for a green card and a flight to the United States.

Mark and Michelle spoke with the State Department about the girl helping with their escape from Iran. That helped to grease the skids and get her preferred treatment and a ticket to America.

"The flight to Bagram AFB will leave in two hours, from there back to S-Cubed?" Asks Mark.

"Yeah, I hope we can get into Andrews again..." Suddenly Michelle's secure phone rings. "Hello? Yes, the operation went well, have you gotten a report on the situation in Iran?"

Mark and Ducky stand listening to Michelle's side of the conversation trying to figure out who is on the other end.

"Ok, we leave for Bagram AFB in a couple of hours. If you have an agency plane waiting for us, then Mark, Ducky and I can be in Washington D.C. by tomorrow morning. Ok, call me if you get more information. Thanks." Then Michelle hangs up the phone. "Well, that was weird. That was Randy Smith wanting to know when I would be back in Washington. The President has called for a Cabinet meeting and he wants me to sit in."

Mark frowns. "Why would he coordinate a Cabinet meeting? And want you there?"

Jihadi White Christmas

Michelle takes a bite of an apple and considers the question. "It is unusual, but then the President has a lot on his plate."

Ducky chimes in, "So what is the word on what's going on in Iran?"

Michelle chucks the apple core into the trash can, then smiles. "It seems the top leadership was assassinated by the Quds force, including the Supreme Leader. A small portion of the Iranian population is mourning the leadership, but those are the diehards who depend on the regime for their livelihood. The majority of the population is pouring into the streets celebrating the potential of regime change. The CIA doesn't know yet what happened to General Aziz and his son. So the government is in chaos."

Mark picks up his go bag and starts for the door. "Our ride is here, I am pretty certain that the VX gas killed everyone in that SUV, but we can't be sure until the bodies show up."

Everyone grabs their bags and follows Mark out the door and onto the tarmac. Mark turns and says over his shoulder with a smile, "It will be nice to get home and some R&R."

Chapter 62

Washington D.C.
September 16th

The President is pacing the thick carpet inside the Oval Office; he has several big decisions to make over the next few days. Kim Jung-Un has been extensively interrogated and all of their secret nuclear sites have been found and beginning to be cleared. The danger from North Korea is over. The clean up is ongoing. Over sixty thousand North Korean troops were killed or injured during the first several days of fighting. Almost two thousand American and South Korean troops were also hurt or killed. The difference was the stand-off weapons that allowed the Allied forces to hit the NKPR without putting their mainline troops in harms way. But now that the

371

ceasefire has been in place, the food deliveries have begun. With overwhelming starvation throughout the countryside, the military is confident that with full stomachs, the population can be pacified.

"Where the hell is Randy?" the President shouts to his secretary.

His longtime secretary peeks her head into the Oval office. "He called to say he wasn't feeling well today. He will be in tomorrow however."

The President shakes his head, "Damn bad time to catch a bug. What about the Cabinet meeting?"

The secretary goes back to her desk and reviews the President's schedule for the week. She comes back into the Oval office and replies, "It is scheduled for 1 pm tomorrow."

"What do we know about Mark Aldin and Michelle Samaha? When are they due back in Washington?"

"I understand they are in-flight now and should be here tomorrow morning. Do you want to see them?"

"Yes, arrange for both of them to come to the White House as soon as they land. I want to thank them personally for their operation and get a first person account."

The secretary acknowledges the request and closes the door, leaving the President to move onto another pressing issue; Iran.

Chapter 63

Washington D.C.
September 16th

George Watkins is sitting in his office daydreaming of the day he is sworn in as President of the United States. His speech will have to be deferential to the late President and Vice President, extolling national unity behind the two major parties and vilifying their enemies. The nation will be in mourning, well maybe the thirty-six percent that voted for him. The rest of the electorate will want to move on, reunify Korea, punish Iran and vilify the traitor Michelle Samaha.

The Speaker of the House smiles. The black flag operation is well planned and hopefully well executed. The only wild card is Randy Smith. That little twerp has been the President's lap dog for the past twelve years.

George takes a sip of his scotch. It's early, but he needs the pick-me-up. Tomorrow is the day the nation will be changed for the better. This President has lucked out so far, his luck is about to run out.

There is a knock and George says, "Come on in Jordan."

Jordan Claiborne enters with a grim look on his face, walking like a man with severe case of the yips.

"Jordan, get a drink and sit down."

The senior Senator from Texas grabs a short glass and plunks in two ice cubes and fills the glass with three fingers of fine scotch. He ambles over to an adjoining couch and sits heavily. "God, I hope I don't have a heart attack before tomorrow."

The Speaker smiles. "Relax Jordan, Randy Smith will do what he has to get your seat."

"Should we meet with him one more time to make sure he will go through with it?"

George sits forward in his comfortable chair. "No, we can't have any contact with him. It might implicate us. Just relax, stop being so paranoid."

"What if the President asks us to be in the Cabinet meeting? How do we refuse the request?"

Speaker Watkins stands and takes a healthy sip of his scotch. "The only people there will be the President, the Vice President, the Secretary of State, the Secretary of the Treasury, the Attorney General, the Chairman of the Joint Chiefs and Michelle Samaha. Randy will make sure her finger prints are on the case, and then he will leave it near her chair and exit the room before the meeting starts. There is a ten minute timer. This will give Randy the opportunity to go to his office and start a meeting of his own."

Jordan nods, "What is the back up plan if Randy fails?"

"If the bomb fails to detonate and they discover the suitcase, then the Secret Service will turn over every rock to find who placed it there. In that case Randy has to go, and go quickly. If the bomb does go off but the President and Vice President are not both killed then Randy has to go. If anything goes wrong and the Cabinet is not destroyed and everyone in that meeting, then Randy has to go. So Randy is very motivated not only to get your seat, but to stay alive.

Jordan chuckles. "Maybe Randy should go regardless of the outcome?"

Rik Thistle

The Speaker refills his glass, and then turns with a smile on his face. "Perhaps you are right."

Chapter 64

S-Cubed Headquarters
September 17th

Mark and Michelle after arriving at Joint Base Andrews are whisked to the S-Cubed headquarters to change clothes and get briefed on what has happened over the past week.

"Let's meet in twenty minutes to talk about the Cabinet meeting this afternoon. I want to give the President the latest INTEL."

Mark and Ducky agree and head for the men's locker room to change and get some food.

Some twenty minutes later the three plus Jonathan Bardsley are huddled in the main conference room pouring over the Iranian operation details trying to summarize the pertinent details into a five minute presentation that Michelle is scheduled to deliver to the President's Cabinet members. This is a big deal; Michelle has never been invited to address the Cabinet.

Mark looks up from his notes. "Ok, I think that this summary will give the Cabinet what they need to know."

Ducky pipes in, "I agree, they don't need to know the operational details just the results."

Michelle is about to speak when Kelly Campos rushes in. "Boss, we might have a major problem."

Everyone looks up at the towering figure in cargo shorts, a MIT Tiddlywinks Team shirt and sandals.

"What have you got Kelly?" Asks Michelle.

The young man suddenly looks very nervous; he is normally always calm and collected. "Well, over the past week I've been monitoring the NSA data, searching for any domestic or international chatter about Iran and designed an algorithm to include a key word search that includes about five hundred words related to the Iranian operation. Over the past couple of days I started getting some hits. But the surprising thing is that it came from a domestic source. The Iranian operation was top secret and tightly controlled. Only a dozen people knew about it."

Kelly sits grabs a handful of M&Ms from the bowl in the middle of the table specifically set out by Michelle for her favorite analyst. "Anyway, I started to look at some of the events, as we call them. One mentioned both you and Mark, then Randy which I assume is Randy Smith the President's Chief of Staff. But it wasn't related to Iran, it was related to the Cabinet meeting this afternoon."

"Who was talking?" Asks Michelle.

"It was a phone conversation between two men; one was named Jordan, the other George. The call was made within the Beltway."

The group sits quietly for a minute considering the information. "Well it was a strange conversation to say the least. Very cryptic. I think someone is planning a coup here in America." Says Kelly.

Michelle looks up suddenly. "A coup? Here?"

Kelly pulls out several sheets of paper. "Here is a copy of the phone conversation, but here is the recording. You tell me."

He slides a sheet to each of the team members, then keys the recorder and it begins:

"Yes?"

"George, this is Jordan. Is there anyone there?"

"No, I am alone sitting in my office working on my second drink."

"Yes, me too. Have you heard from Randy?"

"Everything is in place. I spoke with him yesterday and he seems to have the balls to pull this off."

"The meeting should take place within a few days. After that, all hell will break loose for a few weeks or even months. You have to be ready to take control."

"Yes, I know. I have an able staff that will be able to pull the government back together. It won't be easy but it's our only shot. Jordan, I'll need your help."

"Of course, of course. I will convene the Senate and we'll pass whatever measures you require to maintain control."

"What about the military? Will they follow new leadership?"

"Absolutely, after an attack by North Korea and Iran? They will be chomping at the bit to kick some ass."

"One major issue might be Mark Aldin, I understand he might be too close to Samaha."

"Ok, I think all future communications should be in person. I'll arrange a meeting with your secretary tomorrow. Good night."

Michelle looks up after hearing the conversation. "Holy Moly, I think this is a phone conversation between Jordan Claiborne the Senator and George Watkins, the Speaker of the House."

Mark speaks up, "Could this be conspiracy to topple the U.S. Government?"

Ducky and Jonathan both say at the same time, "Seems like it."

384

"Clearly they are referencing Randy Smith the President's Chief of Staff. Would he really conspire behind the President's back?" Asks Michelle.

Mark moves to the white board and starts writing. "Here are the key phrases; 1. Everything is in place, 2. the meeting should take place within a few days, 3. pull the Government back together, 4. will the military follow new leadership, 5. a major issue might be Mark Aldin and Samaha."

Mark sits and looks at the white board. "Seems pretty clear they are planning something. So I think we agree that the Senator and Speaker are the two talking, agreed?"

Everyone in the room nods.

"Ok, everything is in place. They have a plan and its operational. Agreed?" They all nod.

"Second, the meeting will take place within a few days. When did this call take place?"

Kelly speaks up. "Yesterday."

"So is there a big meeting schedule for the President?"

Michelle leans forward. "The Cabinet meeting this afternoon. I just got the meeting roster. The President and the Vice President plus several of the other key Cabinet members."

Mark stands. "Ok, if I was going to topple the government, I'd have to take out both the President and Vice President at the same time. There are very few events where both people are present."

Michelle moves to the white board and writes; *President, Vice President, Speaker of the House. The Presidency line of session.*

Suddenly Michelle understands the motivation. "President Baker is elected as an Independent, making both major parties losers. It stops the hundred years of two party rule. Each party basically trades power each eight or so years. Almost every person elected gains wealth during their term or terms and then can trade the knowledge and influence for very lucrative jobs in the private sector once they are out of power. But some don't want to lose that power. They are driven to higher and higher position. I think George Watkins is one of those people. If the President and Vice President are killed in an attack of some kind, then he can pick up the pieces and unite the country under his leadership."

"Especially after the EMP attack and aftermath." Says Mark.

"So how would they do it? It would have to be a nerve agent release or a bomb. Nothing else would do the job and make sure nobody survives the attack." Says Jonathan.

Michelle looks at her team. "Well, if this is the plan, then we have just four hours to confirm it and try to stop it. Let's get to work."

Chapter 65

White House
September 17th

Randy Smith is nervously sitting in his office. In less than two hours at the Cabinet meeting, everything will change. He glances down at the government-issued briefcase beside his desk. It contains some papers forged on Michelle Samaha's S-Cubed letterhead.

In the aftermath of the explosion, every minute detail will be examined by the FBI. A shard of paper discovered will lead them to the conclusion that Michelle Samaha, a Muslim, was willing to sacrifice herself to kill the President and Vice President.

Randy smiles. Senator Smith, that sounds right. He'll have to move down to

Texas, maybe develop a Texas drawl. Trade his wingtips for cowboy boots and start eating BBQ rather than Sushi. It was a fair trade for the power and prestige of the Senate. After all several current and former politicians moved to a state specifically to run and become a Senator.

There is a knock at the closed door. "Yes" says the Chief of Staff.

Michelle enters Randy's office with a smile on her face.

Randy is surprised to see her but recovers quickly. "Hi Michelle, congratulations on your Iranian operation."

Michelle walks slowly around his office examining the awards and commendations up on his wall. This was the first time Michelle has been to see Randy in his office.

"Nice office."

"Thanks, so to what do I owe this visit?"

Michelle completes her short tour when she spots the briefcase sitting alongside his desk. Michelle then sits in one of the leather chairs opposite the President's Chief of Staff. "I wanted to give you a quick summary of my presentation that I'll give at the Cabinet meeting at 1 pm. Will you be in the meeting?"

Randy sits back. "I have not been invited. Cabinet staff only plus of course you."

Michelle smiles. "Well, here is the summary of the Iranian op. Very successful if we were able to eliminate Aziz and his son. We'll know more by tomorrow. Their coup attempt failed."

Randy nods looking over the summary.

Michelle gets up and reaches for the hard-sided four wheeled silver briefcase. Randy looks up with shock on his face.

"Nice briefcase. Is it a TUMI?"

Randy is watching her hand holding the briefcase; the button to trigger the bomb just an inch from her fingers. "Ah, yes, the President gave it to me. He personally went to the TUMI store in Georgetown to get it."

"Very nice. Well, I have to get back to the office, then back to the White House for the Cabinet meeting. I guess you'll be there, right?"

"Yes, I'll be there with the President until the meeting starts. I have my own meeting with the Labor Secretary and his staff at the same time."

Michelle nods. "Ok, see you there." She puts the briefcase down and walks out of the office.

Randy takes a deep breath. Then he looks over at the briefcase and smiles. Michelle just gave him a huge gift; her fingerprints on the device that will assassinate the President and Vice President.

Chapter 66

White House
September 17th

The President and Michelle emerge together from the Oval Office. Randy Smith was just walking into the secretaries' office area to speak with the President.

"Mr. President, I was just coming to see you." Says the Chief of Staff.

"Sure Randy, walk with us. We are heading to the Cabinet room for the meeting. What do you have on your mind?"

The trio walks together the short distance from the Oval Office to the Cabinet room. Randy is pulling his briefcase behind him.

"Ah, I just wanted to discuss your schedule for next week."

The President smiles and claps his hand on Randy's shoulder. "Sure, but lets do that after this meeting, ok?"

"Sure. It can wait."

The group rounds a corner and enters the Cabinet room. Inside the assembled leaders all stand. Randy follows the President to his place at the front of the long mahogany table. Next to him is the Vice President. Randy hits the button and puts his briefcase down between the two men as he shakes the V.P.'s hand. The briefcase is under the table and is unseen by both men.

"Ok, lets get this meeting going, it's almost 1 o'clock, I want to keep this meeting on time."

Randy moves towards the door.

"Randy would you like to stay?"

Randy turns surprised, "I am sorry Sir, I have a meeting scheduled with the

Labor Secretary and his staff for five minutes from now."

The President nods. "Ok, that will be all Randy, thank you."

As Randy closes the door, the President looks at Michelle and smiles.

Randy Smith comes into his office and finds Mark Aldin, Ducky Duckworth and the Attorney General seated at his conference room table.

Randy looks around expecting to see the Labor Secretary and his staff; not the CIA. "What are you doing here?"

Mark smiles. "Randy, would you please sit down. We have something that you need to know."

Confused, Randy Smith takes a seat. "What is this all about?"

Mark folds his hands on the conference table and looks at the Chief of Staff. "We have credible information that there is a plot against the life of the President."

Randy shows true shock on his face. How could they have found out? Do they know who is involved? "An assassination plot? Who is involved?"

Mark notices Randy glance at his wrist watch. It is now 1:07 pm.

"Well, we have several suspects but it is clear that the highest levels of the government are involved."

Mark can see a sheen of sweat forming on Randy's upper lip. "How high?"

Just then Michelle Samaha enters Randy's office. He is surprised but then terrorized as he see's what Michelle is pulling.

"Randy, you forgot to grab your briefcase when you left the Cabinet meeting. Here it is." Michelle says as she wheels it into the middle of the room.

Randy glances at his watch again; 1:09 pm. He visibly starts to shake. "Ah, I think we should move this meeting to the Roosevelt Room."

Nobody moves. "Why is that Randy?"

Now he is starting to panic. "We have to get out!" Randy starts to run towards his office door.

Mark springs to his feet and grabs Randy. While the two struggle, Mark winds up and hits the man with a well placed punch that breaks his nose. Randy drops like a sack of potatoes.

Michelle moves to the briefcase. "We found out about your plot from the DNI, Andy Cobb. When you left the Cabinet meeting, the bomb squad came in and secured the device and we exchanged your briefcase for this one." Michelle says resting her hand on the case. "Andy has been the Government's Trojan horse within

397

the CABAL for the past twenty years, ever since the CABAL tried to assassinate Regan. He reported to the President about your plans. All of the members who voted for the assassination of the President have been arrested."

Just then the door bursts open and three large FBI agents enter. "Randy Smith, you are under arrest for the plot to assassinate the President and Vice President of the United States."

The former Chief of Staff is handcuffed and looks towards Michelle and Mark. "You have no proof."

Michelle smiles. "Randy, we have already arrested George Watkins and Jordan Claiborne in the conspiracy. They have confessed to the plot. All of you will be executed for treason."

With that, the FBI agents march Randy Smith out of his office and into a

Jihadi White Christmas

waiting blacked out FBI SUV parked just
outside the White House.

Chapter 67

The Oval Office
September 17th

The President of the United States is sitting behind the Resolute desk smiling, Michelle and Mark are sitting opposite him. The late afternoon sun is just starting to set through the windows behind him.

"I want to thank you both again for all you've done for your country and for my family. We still have some significant challenges facing us, but without your hard work and valor, the country would be in chaos."

"Thank you Mr. President, but we are just doing our jobs." Says Michelle.

"Well, I imagine you are both exhausted."

"Yes sir, we have been in the debrief with the Attorney Generals office most of the afternoon, giving them the details of how we discovered the conspiracy and it was collaborated by Director Cobb. We haven't been able to get home yet for a shower and some chow." Adds Mark.

The President nods. "It is hard to believe that it's been just three weeks since the HEMP nuclear attack. Electricity has been restored at least intermittently throughout the country, food and water supply lines have been established, telephone service is up and running, two of the three major networks have begun broadcasting and banks are opening. All in all it looks like the country has survived the most devastating attack in it's history. It will take months, maybe years for everything we took for granted to come back to normal, but the United States stands strong.

The President stands and extends his hand. "Thank you both for your service and your friendship."

After shaking hands, Michelle asks, "So what is the latest in Iran?"

The President smiles. "I received a telephone call from the new moderate leader of Iran. With the Supreme Leader and the Mullahs all dead, the students rushed into the streets and protested the theocracy. The Republican Guards fought back, but without General Aziz they just didn't have the same leadership. The military decided to step in and they disarmed the IRGC and Quds Force while restoring peace."

The President pauses for dramatic effect, and then says.

"They are scheduling fair elections for six months from now and I am confident that the good people of Iran will elect moderate leadership that we can work with.

I have pledged U.S. support of the new government and elimination of the sanctions. That should significantly help their economy and therefore the people of Iran. They also agreed to talks to eliminate their nuclear weapons program. They saw what we did to North Korea and they are concerned about Israel perceiving them as a nuclear threat. I told them that if they dismantle their nuclear program, I will hold peace talks at the White House between them and Israel."

Mark speaks first. "Wow, that is great! The Persian people deserve a fair government; they have so much potential that hasn't been allowed to flourish."

"I hope this all happens so that we won't have to worry about a nuclear war in the Middle East." Says Michelle.

The President adds, "Also we destroyed three new ICBMs in the Syrian desert today. All the other ICBMs were seized by the new government and will be dismantled. The President smiles and says, also the leadership of Iran told us that General Aziz and his son were both killed by a VX attack."

"So what are your plans? You both deserve a long vacation."

Mark looks at Michelle and smiles. "I was hoping we could "hijack" an Agency plane, then fly to L.A. to make sure my ex-wife and daughter are ok. I spoke to them last night and they survived the worst of the blackout. Apparently it was tough on both of them. They had to kill a couple of guys who broke into their home, and also a neighbor who I never liked but never thought he would attempt to rape and kill my ex-wife and daughter."

Michelle and the President look shocked. "They killed three people?"

Mark nods. "Sure glad I taught Mary how to shoot and left two guns with her for self-protection. I'd still like to see them in person to make sure they are safe. Then if I still have the agency plane, then I am planning to fly to New Zealand."

With that, Mark turns to Michelle and drops to one knee. "Michelle Safiya Samaha, will you marry me?"

Michelle covers her mouth with surprise, and then says "Yes!"

The President smiles, knowing what Mark had planned.

Michelle looks at the President. "Well, I guess I am going to L.A., then on to New Zealand too. We are going to be married!"

The President grins. "I thought that might happen, but I wasn't sure if Mark was receiving all the signals. Glad he did."

The couple kiss and Mark slips an engagement ring on Michelle's finger. "I always wanted to propose in the Oval Office."

The President laughs. "How long will you be on your honeymoon in New Zealand?"

Mark looks at Michelle, and then says. "For a life time."

Then Michelle turns and says with a smile, "unless something catastrophic happens and you need us..."

#   #   #

The End

www.ingramcontent.com/pod-product-compliance
Lightning Source LLC
Chambersburg PA
CBHW051935240626
47153CB00005B/1501